MAKING WAVES

LOBSTER BAY 3

MEREDITH SUMMERS

SUMMARY

Maxi's life is about to change but not in the way she expects...

Maxi Stevens is at a crossroads. Things between her and James haven't been the same since their kids left the nest. When she finds proof that indicates he may have strayed, she strikes out on her own. James's infidelity has a silver lining, though. Maxi can finally do all the things James wouldn't approve of, like pursuing her lifelong dream of becoming an artist.

But everything is not as it seems. James wants Maxi back and will do anything to win her over. He'll even beg Maxi's best friends, Claire and Jane, for help. Will they want to team up with someone who they think has done their friend wrong?

Jane Miller has her own problems to deal with. She's trying to satisfy the demands of a bridezilla whose outbursts could ruin the first wedding at Tides. The success of the wedding is critical for the survival of the inn that has been in her family for four generations. Luckily she has her sister, Andie, to help out.

Everyone is surprised that Andie is still in Lobster Bay. She didn't think she'd still be here, either, but she's found a few reasons to stick around... at least for a little while. It's not too late for her to go back to her job as an antiques appraiser in NYC and make that one big discovery she's always dreamed of. Does Lobster Bay have something even better to offer?

Jane's new relationship with Mike Henderson hits a snafu, Andie makes a startling discovery, and things come together for Maxi with a happy ending she never would have predicted.

This book can be read as a standalone story, but it will be a lot more fun if you read books one and two first as you will get more background details about some of the characters in this story.

CHAPTER ONE

*S*he was supposed to be the one that had her act together, Maxi Stevens thought as she picked at her bran muffin and pretended to pay attention to the conversation she was having with her two best friends, Jane Miller and Claire Turner. They were at Sandcastles, the bakery and café that Claire owned, seated outside at a cozy café table with steaming mugs of coffee, a plate of Claire's delicious pastries on the table, and Jane's golden retriever, Cooper, at their feet.

The summer morning was bright with sunshine, the warm air spiced with the salty scent of the ocean just one street over, the café abuzz with the murmur of conversation from patrons.

But Maxi didn't notice any of that. Not the vibrant purple, red, and pink flowers that overflowed the large planters separating the café area from the foot traffic, not the colorful awnings hanging above the windows of the quaint shops in the seaside town, and not even the familiar bitter, earthy taste of the dark roast coffee that Claire had brewed just the way Maxi liked it.

Her mind was too busy trying to process the horrible revelation about her husband, James, to notice the everyday things in her hometown that usually brought her comfort and happiness.

How could she have been so stupid? Sure, things had been strained between them, but Maxi had assumed it was a natural adjustment, since their youngest had just moved away to college.

But that was before she'd found the card with the woman's number in his pocket.

And not just any woman either. The number and name were those of Sandee Harris, the very women *Claire's* husband had cheated on her with years ago. Sandee was a realtor in town, so at first blush, it might make sense that James had her card—except she and James weren't in the market for any real estate. And the number was handwritten. Sandee had her *business* number printed on the front of the card, so what was up with the handwritten one on the back?

"...and she wants us to make the floral arrangements with ribbons to match the exact shade of the bridesmaid dresses." Jane turned to Maxi, her side-swept silver bangs fluttering in the breeze, blue eyes inquisitive. "Don't you think that's a little too matchy-matchy?"

Maxi's heart swelled at her friend's confidence in her design abilities. The wedding at Jane's family's inn, Tides, was very important to Jane. It was part of her initiative to get the family business back on track and the very first wedding she'd ever hosted there. The reviews and referrals from this one wedding could have a profound impact on the future of Tides. Jane was gambling everything on that future, not only because the inn had been in her family for four generations but also because she needed the money to pay for her mother's care at Tall Pines, the area's foremost memory care facility.

Maxi considered the question carefully. "I think it could be okay as long as everything that has to do with the wedding isn't that same shade and you don't mind finding more ribbon. Have you already bought some?"

"We were going to do it all in white. White roses, baby's breath, white ribbon, a white tea candle inside clear glass. So we bought the supplies, I made one up and sent a picture, and she complained about the white." Jane rolled her eyes.

Maxi wrinkled her nose. "Sounds like she wasn't too nice about it."

"Andie called her a bridezilla." Jane pulled a piece of fabric out of the pocket of her jean shorts. "She sent me this swatch of the bridesmaids' gowns so I could match."

Maxi took the small piece of sky-blue fabric. "Pretty

color. Sounds like it wouldn't be too bad to just get some ribbon over at the fabric store."

Jane nodded. "She also wanted tall candles with stripes to match a lighthouse but in this same blue color."

Maxi pressed her lips together. "Oh. That sounds like a bit more work."

"And she's demanded that I make the frosting of the sandcastle cake the same shade." Claire cut into a chocolate croissant that was on the platter. A thick blob of chocolate oozed out of the middle as she put half on her plate. Cooper's ears perked up at the sound of the knife on the plate, but he didn't move from his spot. "How am I going to make an exact match? It's not like I have a full palette of colors to work with when mixing frosting."

Claire's pride and joy were the cakes she made that were shaped like sandcastles and covered with sugar-coated fondant that resembled beach sand. She was probably regretting agreeing to provide them as wedding cakes for the beach-themed weddings at Tides right about now.

"Oh no. Surely she doesn't expect the shade to be exact." Maxi looked down at the fabric swatch in her hand. "I mean, a ribbon is one thing, but painting the candles and the frosting is another."

"She's very specific, and when we talked on the phone, I could hear her mother in the background making things worse," Jane said. "I need this wedding, but I almost wish I'd never gotten myself into this. Hopefully all brides don't act like this."

"It's almost as if she's making it as difficult as possible to pull off the wedding of her dreams." Claire stuffed an auburn lock back into the barrette at the back of her head where she secured her thick shoulder-length hair.

"Maybe that's what she is doing. Subconsciously, I mean. Who could blame her? Being married isn't all it's cracked up to be," Maxi blurted out.

Ooops... Now why had she said that? Too late to take it back now. Claire and Jane had stopped talking and were staring at her, so she'd have to come clean. But not all the way—she didn't actually have solid proof that James was cheating, and she owed it to him not to accuse him until she did.

"Is there something you're not telling us?" Jane asked.

Maxi felt bad. Usually the three of them told each other *everything*. But Claire's new relationship with Rob Bradford was going so well, and Jane had her own problems with her mother, plus a budding romance of her own. Maxi hadn't wanted to bring them down with her problems. Besides, she didn't have anything concrete to say. Still, she supposed she had to say something now.

"Not really. It's just that things have been weird between James and me for a while now."

Claire put her hand lightly over Maxi's. "I've noticed you mentioned a few things over the past weeks, but I didn't want to pry. Tell us what's wrong. You know we have your back no matter what."

The comfort of her friends' support buoyed her, and Maxi took a deep breath. "It's just that he's never home anymore. I can't tell you how many cold dinners I've thrown in the trash."

"Where is he? At work?" Jane peeled the wrapper off a corn muffin and slathered it with butter.

"So he says."

Jane and Claire exchanged a look.

"I suppose as the bank president, he does have a lot of work to do," Claire said.

"He's become distant. We hardly ever talk." Maxi wrapped her hand around the coffee mug as if seeking comfort from its warmth. "When the kids were home, the dinner conversation was filled up with what they'd done. What they were learning in school, sports, that sort of thing. Now that it's just me and James, apparently there is nothing to talk about."

"I think that's natural." Jane pinched off a tiny piece of muffin and fed it to Cooper. "You focused on the kids all your lives. Now that it's just the two of you, things are different. I bet James came home late a lot before too. You just didn't notice as much because of the kids."

"Yeah, and you were busy driving them to sports and activities. Now you have a lot more time on your hands," Claire added. "You could be reading too much into things if you're focusing on what is or isn't going on between you and James. Maybe you should pick up a hobby."

"Great idea," Jane said. "I know you've been sketching on napkins, but what about taking it even further? You used to love painting when we were in high school. Didn't James suggest that you do that anyway?"

"He did, but..." Maxi's voice trailed off. She didn't want to say what she was thinking, that James had suggested she take up painting again to keep her busy and distracted so she wouldn't notice what he was doing. Claire and Hailey—Claire's assistant at the bakery—had said their cheating husbands had done that. And why would he suddenly want her to start painting? She'd put aside her ambitions to become an artist so she could focus on raising the kids, and even when they got older and she had more time, James had discouraged her creative tendencies. Back then, he was working his way up in the bank. He wanted to become president someday and didn't think being artsy was befitting of a bank president's wife. Appearances were important to James.

"Have you talked to him?" Claire signaled to Hailey, who was circling the area with a coffeepot to top off people's cups. "Maybe you should tell him how you feel, suggest some things that you could do together that would bring you closer again. Or some things that would give you goals and a purpose."

"I've mentioned a few things, but James acts dismissive of them. I've mentioned getting a pet before, but he doesn't want animal hair on his suits." Maxi bent down and scratched Cooper behind the ears. She loved animals and had broached the subject of a dog or cat a few times. James wasn't interested, so she supposed she'd have to make do with Jane's dog, Cooper, and Claire's cat, Urchin. "I saw the most adorable kittens at the animal shelter the other day. Little balls of fluff, one white and one black, but when I approached James, he basically just changed the subject."

"Maybe he needs time to think about a pet. It's a big commitment. What about some things the two of you can do together?" Claire persisted.

Maxi shrugged. "We don't have a lot of the same interests anymore. James is mostly interested in work." *And apparently Sandee Harris.* "I've mentioned a few things to him. A trip to Myrtle Beach. Oh, and ballroom dancing."

A snort came from behind the planter, and Sally Littlefield, Lobster Bay's favorite handywoman, peeked around the side. She had her work overalls on and a paintbrush in her hand as she was apparently giving the planters a fresh coat of paint.

"Sorry, but I can't picture stodgy James taking ballroom dancing."

"Yeah, he didn't seem too keen on it," Maxi said.

Sally rested her brush on the open can of paint and stood, wiping her hands on the rag hanging from the loop at her hip. A thick braid of gray hair hung over one shoulder. Sally was on the other side of seventy, but that didn't slow her down. As one of Lobster Bay's most sought-after handywomen, she was known for her meticulous work and unsolicited advice. "I couldn't help but overhear. Maxi, you've invested a lot in your marriage. You have kids, a home. You can make it work. Maybe you just need a little break."

Hailey had made her way over to the table, and Maxi held up her cup while she thought about what Sally had just said. Maybe she *did* just need a break, but what exactly did that entail?

"How are you ladies this morning?" Hailey asked as she made the rounds with the coffee, serving those at the table as well as Sally, who had a mug stashed next to the paint.

"Good. How about you? How's Jennifer?" Maxi liked the young single mother. They all did and had taken her under their wing, acting somewhat as pseudo-grandmothers to her twelve-year-old daughter Jennifer. Hailey had had a rough time. Her husband had lost all their money then cheated on her. She didn't have much for family, either, just a grandfather, so Maxi, Jane, and Claire tried to treat Jennifer a little specially.

"We're good. Jennifer is doing a summer camp and

—" Hailey's apron pocket erupted in song, and Hailey pulled out her phone. She frowned at the screen. "It's Gramps. He never calls. I better take this."

Hailey put the coffeepot on their table and stepped around the planter, the phone to her ear.

"I hope nothing's wrong." Jane's gaze followed Hailey, her words echoing Maxi's thoughts.

On the other side of the planter, they could see Hailey's shoulders droop as she talked into the phone. A few minutes later, she came back to the table for the coffeepot, her face tight with worry.

"I hope that wasn't bad news," Claire said. "I can handle things if you have to leave."

"I don't have to leave. It was about Gramps's cottage. The one on the beach." She looked at them, and they nodded. Hailey's grandfather wasn't a rich man but did have a small run-down cottage on a more isolated part of the beach that had been in his family for generations. Maxi remembered Hailey saying one time that he could barely pay the taxes and had to rent it out. He didn't want to let it go—too many childhood memories that he wanted Jennifer to also experience.

"What about it?" Jane asked as Hailey bent down to pet Cooper.

"It's getting really run-down, but he's been able to rent it every summer. Except the people that rented it this year took one look and refused to stay," Hailey said.

"Oh no. Can he get someone else?" Claire asked.

"Unfortunately not. The people sent pictures to Airbnb, and they terminated his listing. Said it wasn't fit to rent." Hailey's expression turned grim. "He needs that money for the tax bill. Now he might have to sell."

"No, he won't. I'll rent it," Maxi blurted out.

All eyes turned to her, and she felt a sinking sensation in her chest. Had she just offered to rent a cottage? What would James say?

"Maxi! What are you going to do with a cottage? You have a gorgeous house on the cliff," Jane said.

"Right. I know. But maybe I can use it as a retreat. I mean, it's right on the beach, and I've always wanted an artist studio or cottage on the beach." Maxi looked down into her coffee mug, away from their shocked gazes. "And besides, things are changing between me and James. It might be smart to have someplace to go."

"Are you sure?" Hailey asked. "It's really run-down. You might not like it."

"I'm sure. Give me your grandfather's number, and I'll call him right away to make arrangements." Hailey rattled off the number, and Maxi put it into her phone. Now that she thought about it, renting the cottage was a great idea. She wasn't sure if she would even tell James. Even though her house on the cliff was gorgeous, she'd always loved being right down on the beach. She could turn it into an art studio. And if Claire was right about her just needing something else to put her mind on, then this would be the right move. She excused herself from the table to call Hailey's grandfather.

Sally frowned and shook her head, her gaze following Maxi. "When I suggested a time-out, I meant like a girls' weekend away, not renting a whole cottage."

❀

"I hope Maxi doesn't do anything drastic," Jane said as she slipped another piece of muffin under the table to Cooper.

She glanced over at the corner of the building where Maxi was on the phone. Today Maxi was wearing one of her more casual outfits, a flowing pale-yellow skirt and white linen sleeveless top. Her silvery-blond hair hung loose just past her shoulders. Normally Maxi had more of a tailored look, which Jane suspected was what James preferred. But lately her friend had been dressing more and more casually. Things were changing with Maxi, and Jane hoped it was for the better.

"Yeah, renting that cottage was kind of sudden. I didn't realize things were that bad, and honestly, it doesn't seem that they are from where I'm sitting. I still remember how it all went down with Peter and me, and unless Maxi isn't telling us everything, things might not be as drastic as they seem." Claire glanced across the street, and Jane followed her gaze.

Claire was looking over at Bradford Breads, no

doubt feeling thankful that she'd connected with the owner, Rob Bradford, and things were going good for them. Jane didn't have any divorce experience to compare with—her husband had died young—but she, too, had a new romance to be thankful for. She hoped Maxi wasn't going to have to go through a painful divorce, but she'd had suspicions of James for a week now. "I thought I saw James with Sandee in one of the cottages on the beach last week when I was walking Cooper. I asked Maxi if they were thinking about buying a cottage, but she knew nothing about it." Jane's gaze drifted again to Maxi, who was still on the phone with Hailey's grandfather. "But I could have been mistaken. I didn't get a good look."

Claire frowned. "You don't think James and Sandee..."

Jane sighed. "I don't know what to think."

Sally, who was now munching on a chocolate chip muffin, brushed some crumbs off her shirt. "Sandee does like to cheat with married men."

Claire made a face. "Yeah, but James? He's as steady as they come."

"And he and Maxi have been together forever." Jane hoped Maxi was just being overly sensitive and that the man she'd seen with Sandee was someone else. But then, relationships could be uncertain. Maybe she'd better take it slow with Mike. She hadn't dated anyone else since Brad died ten years ago, and she didn't need another heartache. Plus she'd only known Mike a few weeks, and if husbands who had been married for decades could dump their wives without batting an eyelash, she had to think of what a guy who'd only been in town for a few weeks would do.

"I'm sure things will work out." Claire had picked up the swatch and was frowning at it. "I just hope I can match this color on the cake."

Jane put her hand on Claire's arm. "Don't stress about it. If you can't match it exactly, she'll just have to understand. I appreciate everything you're doing for me."

Claire smiled. "Hey, whatever it takes. We're going to pull this wedding off. At least you have Andie here to help."

The mention of Jane's sister made her smile. They'd been close as kids, but when Andie left after high school, they'd gradually drifted apart. Andie hardly ever came back to Lobster Bay, but now that their mom's dementia had progressed to the point that she had to be in a facility, Andie had come back. It did look like she was sticking around, at least for a while. Their relationship was coming back to what it used to be, but there was still a lot of work to be done in that department. Jane didn't dare get her hopes up. "Andie has been a big help. Both with Mom and the wedding."

"Isn't that her over there?" Claire waved to someone

behind Jane. "Should we have invited her to our morning coffee catch-ups?"

Jane turned to see her sister coming toward them. Though Andie was four years older than Jane's forty-eight years, she looked about ten years younger with her long dark hair and slim figure. Today she was wearing oversized sunglasses, a black tank top, and tan capris. Her style was more reflective of New York City, which made sense as that was where Andie had lived most of her adult life. "I doubt she'd be interested in that, and besides, she might not even still be here the next time we have one."

"There you are! Do you have that blue swatch? I'm going to the fabric store and thought I'd try to match some ribbons for the centerpieces." Andie stood on the other side of the three-foot-tall planters that separated the café from the main sidewalk. Her position on the opposite side of the planters was further evidence to Jane that she didn't want to join in on their morning coffee routine.

Claire held it up. "It's right here." She stood and leaned over to pass it to Andie. "Can I get you a coffee? Some pastry?" She pointed at the plate.

Uncertainty flicked through Andie's gaze. "Oh... thanks. Um... I guess I'd better not. I have a lot of work to do today."

Jane stood. "We're just about done here anyway. I'll go with you to the fabric store if you'd like."

Andie smiled. "That would be nice."

Jane stood and grabbed Cooper's leash. "Thanks for coffee." She glanced over at the corner of the building where Maxi was still on the phone. "Say bye to Maxi for me and tell her I'll message her later."

Andie glanced back at Sandcastles as she and Jane walked toward the fabric store. Claire's invitation had been tempting. The mugs of steaming coffee, the plate of pastries, the camaraderie. They'd never asked her before, and she wasn't sure if Jane wanted her horning in. If anyone should invite her, it should be Jane, so Andie had declined.

Granted, she'd only been in town for three weeks, and how long she'd remain was uncertain. The fact that she was still here was a surprise to everyone, including Andie. She hadn't expected it to feel so much like home, and spending time with her mother at this critical time of her health was important.

But there wasn't much for her here in Lobster Bay. Even at middle age, Andie wanted to do something important, and she'd worked hard to become one of the top antique appraisers at Christies. She couldn't just throw that all away, which meant she'd have to go back to New York. The best antiques were in the big city, weren't they?

"Do you think we're being too accommodating for this wedding?" Jane asked as they turned down School Street toward the section of stores off main where the small fabric shop was located.

"No. This wedding is important—critical, even. We need to get the good reviews from it. Plus I think that's the way it goes with customers. And really, she hasn't been asking for *too* much. It's all easy fixes."

Jane sighed. "I suppose so. She seems sort of entitled when we talk on the phone."

"Yeah, wait until she actually gets here." Andie knew from dealing with clients on antique estates that they could be a little over the top. Would she even be here when the bride arrived? Some of the guests had booked rooms starting the day before the wedding, but that was still a week away. She couldn't leave Jane to deal with that all by herself, so of course she'd be staying at least that long.

"The thought of all the guests and the wedding coordination almost has me breaking out in hives. I hate dealing with the people. You're much better at that than I am." Jane shot a hopeful sideways glance in Andie's direction.

Andie laughed. "I'll deal with the check-ins, and you can hide in the kitchen with your spreadsheets and accounting formulas. On the bright side, the inn is fully booked, and we're getting reservations for after the wedding too."

"Someone even inquired about a fall wedding."

"See, things are picking up!"

"Mrs. Weatherlee is checking out tomorrow."

"She is? I'm going to miss her. Seems like she's been there forever."

"I know, right? But we can use the room for the wedding guests. I had to turn a few away because we're booked."

Andie slowed. "Oh, that's great we're booked, but I just realized that I'm taking up a room that a paying guest could have."

Andie was staying in the old room she'd always stayed in as a kid when their grandparents ran the inn. When she'd arrived, the inn had only one guest, and she'd thought nothing of taking up a room.

She couldn't find a more permanent place, though, as she'd have to sign a lease. "I'm sorry. I never considered that. I could book into a hotel or Airbnb."

Jane made a face. "Don't be silly. You're helping me out a ton. It's only one room."

"Okay, if you're sure."

"Of course. I need my sister staying with me."

Andie glanced away. She didn't want to see that Jane looked happy at having Andie stay with her, because it made it that much harder to think about leaving. She glanced at the traffic moving slowly down the street. It was peak summer season, and tourists flocked to town, jamming up the narrow roads and causing traffic to the beach to come to a standstill. The coastal town had been designed for fishermen, not tourists, but that was part of its appeal.

She spotted Mustangs, Toyotas, even a cute white-and-red Mini Cooper, but no black truck like her ex Shane Flannery drove. Not that she was looking for him. What they'd had was over and done with decades ago. She'd moved on. But ever since she'd run into him doing repair work at Tides, thoughts of him kept randomly cropping up. Probably guilt over the immature way she'd broken things off back in high school. Probably better if she didn't run into him again.

Taking her mind off the traffic—and Shane—she looked at the swatch again. "I was thinking maybe we should get Maxi to help with the centerpieces. She might have some good ideas." Andie had worked with Maxi on the bathhouse they'd had to build at Tides in order to get permits for the wedding and had enjoyed the collaboration. Maxi was smart and had a good eye for design and style. *Unlike Jane*, Andie thought, eyeing her sister's simple gray T-shirt and faded jean shorts. Jane was plain vanilla.

"That's a great idea. I think Maxi needs to keep busy. She's a recent empty nester." Jane's voice held undertones of a possible other reason Maxi might need to keep busy.

"Yeah, I got a sense that things were a little off at home when I worked with her on the bathrooms."

"You could say that. I think Maxi is really taking the change to heart, and well... to tell the truth, I'm afraid she might do something drastic."

Andie was surprised. "Like what?"

Jane lowered her voice. "She just rented a cottage on the beach. Said it could be for an art studio, but I wonder..."

"She is a good artist." Andie had seen some of Maxi's napkin sketches, and they were quite good. But she wondered about the cottage rental too. Jane made it sound like she thought Maxi might be making too much of her marital troubles, but Jane didn't have any experience with that sort of thing. While Andie had never been married, she had plenty of experience with what happened when relationships soured. If Maxi was going as far as to rent a cottage, there might be more to the situation than Jane knew.

Andie had been too ashamed to admit to her sister that for the past few years, she'd been having an affair with a married man. Of course, Doug had said he was separated, but Andie had discovered that wasn't exactly the truth. It was good luck for Andie that he'd moved on. She wasn't even upset that he hadn't messaged or called her since she'd been in Lobster Bay.

But from that experience, she knew the signs of cheaters. And if Maxi was doing something drastic, like moving out of her house, then Andie thought she might suspect her husband was one. Maybe she was too embarrassed to tell Jane, or maybe she had only suspicions and not positive proof. Either way, Andie felt the bond with Maxi tighten. If Maxi was going through something like that, then Andie wanted to be there to support her.

CHAPTER TWO

*H*ailey wasn't kidding when she'd said the cottage was run-down. The small hundred-year-old structure was covered in cedar shingles turned gray from years of sunshine and salty sea air. The blue shutters were present but faded.

Inside, it looked like nothing had been done in decades. The kitchen had plain wooden cabinets painted white with plenty of dirt marks near the knobs. A little bit of elbow grease would fix that. What elbow grease wouldn't fix were the broken drawer and the holes in the worn linoleum that looked like it had been there since 1940.

One of the walls was down to the studs. The bathroom was functional but rusty, and the bedroom at least had a fresh coat of cheery yellow paint. The old-fashioned brass bed was charming. A few throw rugs, a comforter, and some pillows would spruce that up.

The living room boasted a brick fireplace and shiplap walls. It was serviceable despite the water stains on the ceiling that indicated a leaking roof.

But the view! Maxi could forgive all the problems inside for the unobstructed view of the cobalt-blue ocean and the stretch of white-sugar sand leading to it. And when you opened the sliding glass door, you could hear the waves. It was everything she'd dreamed of.

"I'll take it." She turned to Hailey's grandfather, Henry, a thin man with a halo of white hair and lively green eyes. He stood stooped over, most likely from years of hard work, but his handshake was firm and his voice strong.

Henry glanced around. "You sure? I can't do any fixing up. Don't got the money."

"I'll do some, if you don't mind. Some minor repairs with my own money." Even though she wasn't moving in, fixing some of the things would help with her creativity. She needed her area to look nice, or it would zap her creative juices.

"With your own money?" Henry looked suspicious.

Maxi laughed. "I know it sounds crazy, but this is exactly the retreat I'm looking for. I'm an artist, and the patio outside would be perfect for setting up my easel. I don't mind fixing a few things if you rent it to me long-term. I'd like to bring in some of my own furniture and accessories, too, if you don't mind."

"I *would* like a long-term rental, and since you're a friend of Hailey's, I guess I can trust you." Henry looked out the door to the sea, his eyes clouding with memories. "You know this place has been in my family for a hundred years. It started off as a fishing shack for my grandpa."

"Hailey mentioned that. I bet you had some great times here."

"Ayuh. Used to collect shells right out there when I was a kid." He turned and pointed at the craggy rocks that stuck up out of the sand at low tide. "And there I'd search for starfish and crabs."

"Those sound like great memories."

"I want Jennifer to have those memories too. That's why I won't sell." Henry stroked his chin. "Place down the beach sold for over a million. 'Course I can't get that. This place needs work. But I just can't bring myself to let it go."

"Of course not. Hailey and Jennifer are welcome to come here anytime while I'm renting."

Henry brightened. "Really? Hailey mentioned you've been really good to Jen. I guess that settles it, then." He took a key out of his pocket and handed it to Maxi. "The place is yours for the summer, even longer if you want it."

Maxi took the key and wrote him a check.

❦

Maxi couldn't believe she'd just rented a cottage on the beach. What would James say? Maybe she wouldn't tell him. After all, he had his secrets. Now she would have hers.

But the more she thought about it, the more she realized that wasn't the right move. She didn't have an income of her own, but James had part of his check deposited in an account with only her name. James had insisted when Maxi gave up working to raise the kids that she have her own money to do with as she pleased. James at least had been generous with that. She'd paid Henry with a check from her account. James would never know she'd rented the cottage.

But if she didn't tell him, she was no better than he was. And, after all, she wasn't one hundred percent sure that he was cheating. And he *had* encouraged her to work more on her art. Maybe he'd be optimistic about this move.

She opened the sliders and stood out on the little patio, breathing the sea air, listening to the waves, envisioning herself out there painting. A sense of freedom came over her. A sense that now, finally, she could have everything she wanted. Her thoughts turned to the two kittens she'd seen at the animal rescue. James didn't want pets in the house, but here...

She dialed Henry's number again.

"Ayuh?"

"Henry, it's Maxi Stevens."

"Changed your mind so soon?"

Maxi laughed. "No, it's just that... Well, I was wondering if I could have pets here in the cottage. Just two kittens." *To start.*

"Pets, eh?" Henry chuckled. "Well, why not? Place can't really get much worse. Have as many as you want."

"Great. Thanks. I'll fix any damage, of course."

Maxi hung up and raced to her car. While she'd been talking to Henry, she'd gotten a text from Jane asking if she'd help Andie with the centerpieces for the wedding. She was looking forward to that, as she'd connected a bit with Andie when they worked on the bathroom project at Tides and liked working with her. She had about an hour to kill before meeting Andie. Just enough time to visit the Lobster Bay Animal Rescue downtown and adopt the kittens.

The Lobster Bay Animal Rescue had the unfortunate location of being right next to the realty office that Sandee worked at. *That's okay*, Maxi thought. She could ignore the realty office altogether. She parked in the town lot and walked down. A familiar car caught her eye.

Her car.

The one James took to work. It was at the curb in front of Sandee's office, and James was in it! What was he doing there? He was supposed to be at work!

She stood frozen on the sidewalk as he pulled away from the curb, heading toward her. She wasn't sure what to do. Wave? Step into the street? Shoot his tires out? She couldn't do the latter, since she didn't have a gun, which was probably a good thing.

She couldn't quite see into the car with the way the sun glared off the windshield, but she could have *sworn* that James had seen her. The car sped up, and when he came in line with her, his head was turned as if to avoid eye contact. Did he think he was hiding from her?

Maxi collapsed onto the bench a few steps down. It was true. James was cheating with Sandee. Apparently a little part of her had hoped that she was just making something out of nothing, but this was proof.

That little lying cheat! Well, he couldn't hide from her for long. Tonight she was going to muster all her anger and courage and confront him. The universe must have been looking out for her when the opportunity for Henry's cottage dropped in her lap. At least she'd have somewhere to go.

She wasn't going to let James derail her plans. She pushed up from the bench and marched into the animal rescue.

There was no one behind the desk, so she rang the

bell. After a few seconds, a middle-aged woman—Marie, her name tag said—came out of a door. "Can I help you?"

"Yes, I was in the other day and saw two kittens. I'd like to adopt them."

"Excellent. We have some paperwork..." Marie went to a filing cabinet and pulled out some papers. "Let's go see exactly which ones you are talking about. We have quite a few cats available."

Marie led Maxi through the glass doors and along the cages. Maxi liked it here. It was clean, and the animals looked well cared for. Maybe she'd volunteer now that she was *free*. She stopped midway down the row at a cage where a fluffy black kitten was curled into a ball. "This is one... and the white one in the next cage."

Maxi stepped to the next cage. It was empty. She turned around, glancing in all the cages. "Where is the white kitten? It was right here the other day."

"I'm not sure. One of the other volunteers might have moved him to another cage, or maybe he got adopted. I've been in the stockroom all morning." Marie frowned and flipped through papers on a clipboard that hung from the bottom of the cage. "Looks like that one got adopted."

"Oh no." Darn! She really wanted the pair. Maxi looked around at the other cages. There were plenty of cats but no other kittens.

"Probably for the best. We feel it's better to just adopt one at a time," Marie said.

"Oh, okay." Maxi supposed that advice was wise. She'd be living alone for the first time, and maybe it was smart to take things slow. "I'll just take this one, then."

"Let's fill out the paperwork, and I'll have someone get him ready." Marie led her back out front. "Now, do you have all the accessories? Litter box, cat food, carrier?"

"No, actually. I guess I can get those and come back."

"Good idea. That will give us time to get him brushed and ready." Marie handed her the paperwork. "Just make the check out to the Lobster Bay Animal Rescue."

Maxi stewed about James the whole time she shopped for cat supplies and all the way to Tides.

Of course she should confront him, but was it possible he'd been somewhere else? Was she jumping to conclusions? There were a dozen shops on that street. He could have been in any of them. But that didn't explain why he'd pretended not to see her.

When she got to Tides, Jane was busy with the food delivery and sent her to meet Andie on the back porch.

As Maxi made her way through the historic old home, she noticed that things were taking shape. Broken spindles in the turned mahogany railing had been repaired. The crown molding above the vintage floral wallpaper had a crisp coat of paint. The hardwood floor gleamed a golden oak.

The back porch was perhaps the most amazing feature of Tides. It was wide enough for tables to be set up and wrapped around to the side of the house. A row of white rockers sat at the railing, facing the magnificent ocean view.

Andie was seated at one of the tables. Candles, ribbon, flowers, and glass containers were spread in front of her.

Cooper bounded up to meet Maxi, and her heart lightened as she bent down to pet him. A bubble of excitement pierced her sour mood as she thought about the black kitten who she'd already named Rembrandt. Soon she'd have a pet of her own.

"Hey, thanks for coming." Andie's smile was genuine.

"No problem. This will be fun." Maxi sat down at the table, and Andie slid a fabric swatch and piece of ribbon over to her.

"Do you think these match? The swatch is from the bridesmaids' dresses."

Maxi held them up and turned to inspect them in the light. She'd seen the swatch earlier, but holding the items together provided the best way to compare. "They're pretty close. Maybe a hair off, but I don't think anyone will notice."

"Okay. Good." Andie proceeded to show her how they were thinking about arranging the centerpieces, but Maxi had a hard time focusing. Her mind was on her confrontation with James. Should she confront him as soon as he got home? What if he stayed out late, as he had so often these past months? Should she call and demand he come home on time? Or should she bide her time so she could move her favorite things out of the house before he knew that she'd discovered his affair?

"Maxi?"

Maxi looked up to see Andie looking at her with concern. "Sorry, what were you saying?"

"I was asking about painting the candles. The bride wants stripes, sort of like a lighthouse. Is there a special paint for candles?"

"Ummm. Yeah, you can buy special acrylic candle paint."

Andie put the candle down and looked at Maxi over the rim of her aqua reading glasses. "Is something wrong? You seem a little distracted."

Maxi sighed. She was bursting to confide in someone, but she felt like such a failure. She'd wanted to say more to Jane and Claire that morning, but admitting it to her best friends was hard. Somehow it seemed easier to talk to Andie. She was practically a stranger, yet they'd bonded when they'd worked on the bathrooms together, and Maxi sensed Andie had experience that might help her.

"Things aren't going great with my husband."

"I've noticed over the past weeks you mentioned a few things. Do you want to talk about it?"

"Sort of." As if sensing Maxi's distress, Cooper came to her side, and she buried her hands in the soft fur between his shoulders. "I think he might be cheating."

Andie's gaze narrowed. "Are you sure?"

Maxi thought about it. All the signs pointed at it, and she didn't want to be the sucker of a wife who buried her head in the sand and waited around.

"I'm fairly sure." She told Andie about the card, the late nights, and how James had avoided eye contact when she'd seen him in the car earlier.

"Ouch, that sounds bad. I'm so sorry, Maxi."

"I haven't mentioned the specifics to Jane or Claire yet. I guess I was hoping that I was making too much of things, but when I saw him parked in front of her office..." Maxi felt guilty for not telling Jane and Claire first, but she'd just sort of blurted things out to Andie.

"Don't worry. I won't mention it to either of them," Andie said. "So what are you going to do?"

Maxi gazed out at the ocean. "I'm not sure. Confront him, I guess. Luckily I rented a cottage... it was going to be an artist studio, but now I might just live there until I figure out more about what I want."

"You're doing the right thing."

Maxi turned back to Andie. The confidence in her tone made Maxi feel like she was on the right track. "You sound pretty sure of that."

"I was in a similar situation but maybe reverse." Andie looked away. "I'm embarrassed to admit that I was the other woman. He'd said he and his wife were separated. Turned out it wasn't actually true."

"On no. Is that why you've stayed here longer than usual?"

"Partly. The other part is that Jane needs help here. I want to see it through and make sure Tides gets back on its feet before I run off." Andie glanced into the house through the French doors, a soft smile flitting across her lips. "And to tell the truth, I'm getting really fond of it here. Suddenly it feels like home in a way it never has before."

"So what happened with the guy?"

Andie shook her head. "Once I started asking about taking our relationship to the next level, he became less interested. Turns out he was still with his wife. Then he just pushed me aside, and last I heard, had taken up with someone else. Still not separated from his wife."

"That's terrible. I'm sorry." *Once a cheater, always a cheater*, Maxi thought. Even if she and James worked things out, he'd probably do it again.

"Don't be. Turns out it was the best thing that could

have happened. Now I can live my best life without him treating me as an afterthought."

Afterthought? Was she just an afterthought now for James? After twenty-seven years of marriage and raising three kids?

Well, she wasn't going to stand for that. She had a cottage on the beach, a new kitten, and a new plan for her art career. Middle-aged or not, she still had plenty of time to live her best life.

CHAPTER THREE

*M*axi was waiting for James with her bags packed when he came home. Her car was full of things she wanted to take with her, including all her art supplies. The suitcase at her side held her favorite outfits. She could get everything else later. She'd picked up the kitten at the Lobster Bay Animal Rescue and set him up in her cottage. At least that was something to look forward to after she confronted James.

When his key finally turned in the lock, she almost chickened out. Almost rushed back upstairs with her bags... but she didn't.

James was in a good mood. He came through the door whistling—smiling, even. *Probably just coming from Sandee's place.*

His smile faded when he saw Maxi's face. His gaze drifted to the bags beside her. He stopped mid-whistle.

"Maxi? What's going on?" He was a good actor because he seemed genuinely confused, as if he couldn't think of a reason why Maxi would have her bags packed. Then again, maybe his confusion stemmed from the fact that he thought Maxi was too naive to figure it out. That thought ratcheted up her anger another notch.

Maxi willed herself to keep calm. "I think you know what's going on."

"Are you going on a trip?"

"No. I expect you're probably relieved and happy that I'm leaving."

"Leaving? But where? For how long?" James still seemed confused, and now he looked appropriately upset, which only made Maxi angrier.

"You don't have to play dumb. I know all about what you've been up to."

"You do?"

Ha! See, he isn't even denying it! "I'm not stupid. All the late nights. The way you don't want to take up any of the things I've suggested..."

"Huh? I've been working at the bank on a project. I figure it would give you time to—"

Maxi cut him off. "Enough! At least give me the dignity of admitting it."

"Admitting what? I still have no idea what you're talking about."

"Seriously? I suppose you're going to deny that was you downtown pretending like you didn't see me as you drove past?"

James's face turned red, a sure sign he was lying. He sputtered, "No. I didn't s-see you downtown. I was at the bank. Well, I went out for a—"

Maxi grabbed the handle of her suitcase, the action cutting off his words. She started toward the door. He grabbed her arm as she walked past.

"Maxi, it's not what you think. Let me explain."

The pleading look in his eye might have stopped her if she hadn't been so angry. But she was on a roll now and didn't want to lose her nerve.

It was now or never.

She jerked her arm away. "I'm sorry, James, but I can't listen to any of your excuses now. Don't try to contact me. I'll contact you when I'm ready."

Maxi opened the door and fled before he could say another word.

James stared at the front door, his brain trying to process what had just happened. Maxi was leaving?

"Wait!" He rushed to the door and flung it open, only to see the taillights of Maxi's car as she peeled out of the driveway.

What in the world was going on?

Maxi had been acting a little strange lately, but he'd never expected something like this. He'd thought she was just bored. He'd tried to encourage her to take up one of her old hobbies, but she'd seemed reluctant. And yes, their relationship had been off, but he put it down to all the turmoil with their last child moving out and the house being empty. It was a big change for Maxi. He'd tried to support her, but truth be told, he had no idea how to do that.

He collapsed on the couch, the sinking feeling growing. Was she really gone? Maybe she just needed some time to think. That was probably it.

But she'd said some odd things. It was almost as if she were mad at him for something. Maybe he shouldn't have worked late so much, but the project he was on could be a big one for the bank, and getting it done early meant he could surprise Maxi with that trip to Europe she'd been hinting about.

But now... would he ever go on a trip with her again?

If only she'd let him get a word in edgewise, he would have told her that. Dammit! He'd never been good at thinking quickly on his feet. That was why he'd pretended not to see her downtown. He'd gotten flustered. And tonight she'd caught him off guard, and he didn't know what to say to her because he didn't want to spoil the surprise.

Speaking of which…

James pushed to his feet and ran down to his car in the garage. He opened the door to the back seat and poked his head in.

"Hey there, little guy. Are you okay?"

Two blue eyes surrounded by snow-white fur blinked out from the mesh front of the cat carrier.

"Sorry. I got waylaid. Come on, we'll get you inside." James reached for the handle of the carrier.

Hiss!

Yikes! He jumped back. The cat sounded angry, probably from being left in the car. He looked back in at it.

"Sorry about leaving you in here so long, but I have good news. This is your new home, Picasso." He'd tentatively named the cat after one of Maxi's favorite artists, but if she wanted another name, that was fine with him. *If* she ever came home to see the cat.

He grabbed the carrier and the bag of cat supplies and brought them into the house. He set the carrier on the floor and looked in the bag, realizing he had no idea what to do with the supplies the lady at the animal rescue place had suggested he buy. He'd expected that Maxi would set everything up.

"Hmmm... litter box. Okay. I guess I need to put the litter in and put it... somewhere." He glanced at the carrier where the cat was crouched down, staring at him as if ready to attack. "Better do that first before I let you out, eh?"

Where would Maxi put the litter box? The bathroom? Probably. The bathroom on the main floor was large, and he set the box up in the corner and poured litter in.

Back out in the living room, Picasso was moving around in the carrier.

Meow!

"Guess I better let you out now." James opened the door and stood back.

Picasso poked his head out, his eyes wide as he looked around the room. He tentatively ventured from the carrier. His body low to the ground, he slinked around the carrier's edges and finally came to the bag with his supplies. He stuck his head in and sniffed the cat food bag then turned an accusing glare on James.

Merooow!

Oh right. Poor guy was probably hungry. James filled one of the new stainless-steel bowls with water, the other with food. Picasso didn't waste any time tucking in.

James watched the cat, wondering what Maxi would think of him. She'd been hinting at getting a pet for months now. James had pretended to dismiss the idea, acting like he didn't want a pet, because he'd wanted to surprise her and see the smile light up her face. He wasn't a big animal person, and all that hair did make a mess on his suits. He was very particular about his appearance, but he'd purchased several sticky rollers that he hoped would help remove any hair. A little cat hair on his suits was worth it if the cat made Maxi happy.

Mew. Picasso had finished eating and trotted over to James. He rubbed against James's leg, leaving a clump of white fur on the bottom of his dark-gray Brooks Brothers suit. James grimaced, but when the cat looked up at him with his wide blue eyes, his heart pinged. The small kitten was pretty cute.

He picked Picasso up, holding him away from his body so he didn't get more hair on his suit. "Don't worry, little guy. We'll get her back."

🐚

Maxi put the last of her clothes away in the small pine bureau in the bedroom and shoved the drawer shut. The cottage was a bit more dilapidated than she remembered it being when she'd looked at it earlier, but she'd brought a cheery yellow comforter and sheet set and a few pieces of wall art to spruce up the bedroom.

Mew! Rembrandt jumped up on the bed and looked at her with his eager grayish-blue eyes.

When she'd returned home from her confrontation with James, she'd found him asleep on top of a pillow on the sofa, already seeking out the most comfortable spot in the cottage. He'd used his litter box and eaten the food she'd put out, too, so apparently he was settling in just fine. Maxi wished she could say the same for herself. It felt weird to be moving into a place of her own after living with James for her entire adult life.

She picked the cat up and tucked him under her chin. His purrs were comforting as she stroked his soft fur and walked to the main room. The kitchen was open to the living room, where she'd placed more pillows and artwork. It was starting to look like home.

Her phone pinged. It was James.

Are you okay? I'm worried.

A surge of regret and uncertainty bubbled up. Had she done the right thing? Could she make it on her own? But then she remembered James driving past her and pretending not to see her, and she became angry.

She didn't want to answer him, but she also didn't want him to keep texting, or worse, calling. She put Rembrandt down and picked up her phone.

I'm fine. Staying with a friend. We'll talk later.

She didn't want him to know about the cottage yet because she didn't want him coming over. This was her retreat, her safe space. The place where she could be the *real* Maxi, the one that had been hidden all these years because she'd always done what James wanted. Always worn the outfits he'd approved of, hosted the executive dinners, and frequented the classier establishments instead of wearing colorful flowing skirts, attending art shows, and hanging out at the artsy bohemian bars and coffee shops that appealed to her.

Sure, she'd have to let him know about the cottage eventually, and they'd have to have a discussion at some point, but right now, it was too raw. She needed time to think.

Outside, the moonlight danced along the waves, and the surf crashed on the beach. She'd already set her easel up out on the patio. Tomorrow she'd start painting as soon as the sun came up.

She uncorked a bottle of wine and poured a glass. Then, picking Rembrandt up in one hand and the wine glass in the other, she stepped out onto the patio, where the ocean breeze and sound of the surf were amplified.

Two chairs were placed at the edge of the patio, and she sat in one. Rembrandt curled up in her lap.

She held the wine glass up and looked down at the cat, who was looking up with trusting eyes. "Here's to a new start for both of us."

CHAPTER FOUR

*a*ndie woke up to a ray of sunlight across her eyes. It took her a moment to remember where she was, since the sun was never so bright in New York City. She wasn't in New York, though. She was in Lobster Bay. She was home.

She rolled over to look out at the ocean. A hint of ocean breeze snuck in from the cracked window. She kept the window open a little at the bottom and the shade up just for that reason.

A feeling of contentment washed over her as she kicked off the crisp sheets, sat up, and stretched. Nothing like waking up to an ocean sunrise. Except the sun had risen a few hours ago, and she'd better get a move on if she wanted to catch her mother at Tall Pines before she took her after-breakfast nap.

Her phone rang with the old-fashioned telephone sound she preferred. It was Susie from work.

"Hey, Susie. How are things going?"

"Eh, okay. We got a few estates in, but Elise seems to be getting all the good projects."

Of course she was. Elise was the new appraiser who apparently had replaced Andie both in status at Christies and also in Doug's personal life. Surprisingly, this last part didn't bother Andie in the least. She was over him.

"You must be learning a lot. I hope it's not too much of a workload." Andie had been training Susie before she left for Lobster Bay on a temporary leave to help get her mother settled at Tall Pines. The younger woman had been coming along, a bit slow but steady. She did feel a little guilty about being absent for so long. It meant the others had to put in more hours.

"I am actually. You'd be proud of me. But I was wondering... when are you coming back?" Susie's voice had taken on a pleading tone. "Elise isn't as nice as you when I have a question."

More guilt as Andie thought about the answer. Prior trips to Lobster Bay had been short, as she'd always wanted to get right back to work. But something had changed. Maybe it was being over fifty now, or maybe it was the peaceful setting, but Andie's interest in going back to Christies was waning with each passing day.

"I'm not exactly sure about that."

"Oh, well, I hope you're having a good time. Things

here are a little weird. I'm mostly on my own, since Elise spends most of her time with Doug."

"She does? Huh, well, look on the bright side. You don't have her nagging at you all day." Elise could act a bit superior, and she was bossy.

Susie laughed. "I know, right? Hey, did you know that Chandler Vanbeck is opening an art gallery in Lobster Bay? I ran into him the other day, and he mentioned it."

"He is? Actually, he was staying here at my family inn last week, and he said he was scouting locations. Guess he must have found one." Andie made a mental note to tell Maxi.

When Chandler had been at the inn, he'd seen one of Maxi's sketches and expressed an interest. He'd even given Andie a card to pass on to Maxi. If he was opening an art gallery here in town, he'd need local artists. This could be just the thing Maxi needed to make a positive change. And after what Maxi had told her yesterday, it sounded to Andie like she was going to need something hopeful to focus on.

"Yeah, he's opening pretty soon too," Susie said. "Well, I guess I'll talk to you later. I just wanted to catch up and see if you had a return date yet."

"Nothing yet, sorry."

"Then I suppose I'll carry on on my own."

Andie hung up and quickly got dressed. The smell

of bacon had started to creep into the room, and she wanted to get some while it was still hot and crisp.

Andie detoured through the dining room on her way to the kitchen. They'd had to repair some of the original crown molding, and she wanted to see how the work was coming along. Sally was standing on a ladder, fitting one of the pieces in. She turned as Andie poked her head in.

"Are you looking for Shane?" Sally snorted then turned back to her work. "He's on another job."

"No! I wasn't looking for him." She really wasn't. Why would she? "I wanted to see how the crown molding came out. Looks great."

Andie hurried on to the kitchen.

"Breakfast smells amazing!" She snatched a piece of bacon from the plate Brenda, the cook, was piling slices onto. She broke a small piece off and tossed it to Cooper, who was sitting by the back door, before taking her own bite. It was delicious, crispy and salty.

"Help yourself," Brenda said half sarcastically. "I have plenty for the few guests we have. I can't wait until there's a full house to cook for."

"You won't have to wait long. Wedding guests will start to arrive soon." Jane sounded stressed instead of happy.

"That's good, isn't it?" Andie said as she grabbed a piece of toast and folded it around another piece of bacon.

Jane sighed. "I suppose it is. It's just all that checking in and dealing with their complaints. I think this wedding is testing my limits with people."

"Don't worry. I'll help with the people part."

Jane's face lit up. "I appreciate that so much, but don't you need to get back to your job?"

Andie frowned. Was that a hint? "Not right away. I want to help out."

"You have no idea how grateful I am. And for helping out with Mom too. It really takes a load off."

Andie checked her watch. "Speaking of Mom, I'm on my way to visit her this morning. You don't need me to do anything for the pictures of the centerpieces you're sending to the bride before I go, do you?" She and Maxi had finalized the design and made up a sample center-piece for Jane to send to the bride and her mother for approval.

"No. Claire and Maxi are coming in a few minutes to work on the pillows, and Claire's bringing a sample of her sandcastle cake so we can compare the frosting to the swatch, if you want to wait around."

This was the first time Jane had included Andie in her plans with her friends. It felt silly and high-schoolish to care about that, but for some reason Andie did. "Darn! I wish I could, but I want to get to Tall Pines before Mom goes in for her nap. You know how tired she gets after breakfast."

"Yep. Right about now I could agree with her."

Woof!

They turned to see Mike Henderson at the back door. Cooper always got excited when he saw Mike. The dog had originally belonged to Mike's grandfather, who now resided in Tall Pines. Cooper had bonded with Jane and ended up at Tides when Mike couldn't keep him in his rental.

"Hi, Mike." Andie motioned for him to come in. "You seem to be a regular here at breakfast. Maybe you should just book a room and move in." Andie couldn't help but tease. Mike and Jane had become more than friends. They thought they were hiding their feelings from everyone, but it was blatantly obvious.

Andie shoved the last bite of bacon and toast into her mouth. Seeing that both Jane's and Mike's faces had turned beet red, now was probably a good time to make her exit. "Gotta run. I want to have some time with Mom before nap time."

Andie ran into Maxi in the foyer.

"Hi, I'm glad I ran into you." Andie paused. Maxi had dark circles under her eyes and looked stressed. "Are you okay?"

Maxi took a deep breath, her eyes misting. "Yes, I suppose. I had it out with James last night."

"Oh no. Did it not go well?"

"It went as expected. Truth is, once I got on a roll, I did most of the talking. I was proud of myself that I didn't buy into his excuses or let him talk me into staying."

"Staying?"

"Yeah, I've moved into that cottage I rented from Hailey's grandfather."

Andie had to give Maxi credit. She didn't waste any time. "Oh, do you want to talk about it?"

Maxi glanced at the key fob in Andie's hand. "It looks like you're heading out."

"I was going to see my mom, but if you need to talk..."

"No, you go ahead. We can catch up later. I'm supposed to meet Jane and Claire anyway." Maxi managed a smile. "Was there something you wanted to tell me, though?"

Of course Maxi would want to unburden herself with her best friends, not Andie. "Do you remember Chandler Vanbeck?"

Maxi's brow furrowed, and she tilted her head. "The art appraiser that was staying here?"

"Yep. He's opening an art gallery here in Lobster Bay soon. Do you still have his card?"

Maxi nodded, a spark of interest in her eyes.

"It might not be a bad idea to give him a call. He could be looking for local talent, and it might give you something positive to focus on." Andie reached out and squeezed Maxi's arm. "I'm here whenever you want to talk."

Maxi nodded. "Thanks. I appreciate it."

They headed their separate ways with Andie feeling a little bit lighter knowing that she could help out a friend in need.

❦

"And he didn't deny having an affair?" Jane looked up from her comparison of the swatch next to Claire's sandcastle cake sample. They were sitting on the back deck at Tides, the three of them at one of the tables and Cooper lying next to the wide stairs that led to the sandy beach. Maxi had just finished filling them in on the events of the previous evening.

Maxi saw concern, compassion, and even a little hint of pity in both her friends' eyes. It had been hard to tell them about her confrontation with James, but now that it was out, she felt relieved. Besides, she needed the support of her friends now more than ever.

"Nope." Well, that wasn't totally true. She hadn't *exactly* mentioned that she suspected an affair. "I didn't come right out and accuse him. I couldn't bring myself to say the words. But I know he lied about pretending not to see me downtown."

Claire clucked in sympathy. She, more than anyone, would know how it felt because Peter had done the same to her. "I understand. It's hard to accuse them. Such a betrayal. Don't worry. I know what you are going through and will help you every step of the way."

"We both will," Jane added.

"Thanks." Maxi's throat was too tight to say more. She cleared it and pointed at the cake sample. "Well, I say we cut this thing up and try it out."

Claire made a face. "Might as well. The color doesn't match the swatch enough. Don't you both agree?"

Maxi and Jane nodded. "Sorry, but it's off by quite a few shades."

Claire cut the small sample into three pieces and handed them out, licking frosting from her thumb. "I'll just have to try again. We may be eating a lot of sample cakes in the future."

Cooper raised his head and looked over.

"Not you," Jane said. "Cake isn't good for dogs."

Cooper put his head back on his paws.

Claire mashed the last of the cake crumbs onto the back of her fork. "How was it sleeping alone in the cottage?"

"A bit scary but also freeing. It's great being right on the beach."

"When do we get to see it?" Claire asked.

Maxi wanted to show her friends the cottage but not until she'd made it a little more presentable. She didn't mind springing for a few minor repairs, especially since it would help Henry out, but mostly she planned to spruce it up with some new decor. And since she was known for her decorating skills, she didn't want her friends to see it until she'd had that chance. "I still have some finishing touches to do on the cottage, You know it's sort of run-down, right?"

"We don't care about that!"

"I know, but I want your first impression to be a good one, so give me a couple of days."

"Of course we will," Jane said. "Let us know when you're ready."

"So what will you do now?" Claire asked. "Are you going to do more painting?"

"Funny you should ask. I need advice on that. I ran into Andie on the way out, and she told me that Chandler Vanbeck, the art appraiser that was here last week, is opening an art gallery in town." Maxi appreciated Andie seeking her out to tell her and her offer to talk about things. She made a mental note to fill Andie in later on everything that had happened with James. She didn't want Andie to think she was brushing her off.

"He was impressed with your work. I bet he'd want to put some of it in a show," Jane said.

Maxi laughed. "I'm not sure I'm ready for that..."

"Didn't he leave a card for you when he left?" Claire asked. "I think that shows he might be interested."

"You should at least call him," Jane suggested. "What have you got to lose?"

Maxi felt a nervous flutter of excitement. Her lifelong dream was to be an artist, to have her work in a gallery. But it was all happening too fast. Too much was going on. Still... she'd be a fool to let this opportunity pass, wouldn't she? "Maybe I will give him a call. We'll see."

"Sounds like we might have a lot to catch up on tonight." Jane picked up the swatch and compared it to the ribbon on the centerpiece again. "How about we meet at Splash? We can find out how Bridezilla liked the centerpieces, and Maxi can update us on her call with Chandler Vanbeck."

CHAPTER FIVE

*A*ndie was getting used to Tall Pines, the memory care facility her mother, Addie, now resided in. It was a nice place, set up to look more like a giant home than an institution. Addie's room had been decorated to resemble the way her room at Tides had always looked. It was clean, comfortable, and since it faced south, always bright with sunshine.

Andie had to admit she was surprised at how well her mother had adjusted. Addie was always happy and interacted with the residents, and just like when she ran Tides, she seemed to keep busy. At Tides it was with guest registration and overseeing the cleaning. Here it was with playing cards and word search. It was a huge relief.

Today Addie had been working on a small puzzle at the table under the window when Andie came in. She turned and smiled, recognition lighting her face. She was having one of her lucid moments, which Andie was learning to treasure more and more. Who knew when those would start to become few and far between?

"Are all the guests at breakfast?" Addie asked. Okay, so maybe she wasn't totally lucid. It wasn't unusual for Addie to think that she was still at Tides, though Andie wondered if that didn't have a lot to do with the fact that they'd replicated her room.

Andie took her hand, frail with skin like parchment. "Jane has everything under control. Don't worry."

"Jane's a good girl. You need to help her."

"I'm trying, Mom."

Addie chuckled. "She is a bit stubborn, I know. But she'll come around. After all, everyone should be able to do what they love."

"And Jane loves running Tides?" Andie doubted that, given the way her sister hated dealing with the guests.

"Oh sure, who wouldn't? But *I* run Tides. Jane is just helping." Addie turned curious eyes on Andie. "And what about you? You love Tides, too, don't you?"

Andie pressed her lips together. She did love the old place. It held most of her fondest childhood memories. Her work on restoring the garden at Tides had been invigorating. She'd loved gardening with her mother as a kid but had gotten away from it with being in the city. She'd forgotten how much she loved plants and flowers.

And being back here had changed her. It had made her see that maybe some things she'd thought were important really weren't.

"I do love Tides, but I also really love antiques. Antiques are my passion. There's something exciting about digging around in old trunks and attics, anticipating an important find." Andie sighed and patted her mother's hand. "But all the good antiques are in the city, so if I want to work in that field, I can't stay in Lobster Bay."

"I wouldn't be too sure about that. These old New England towns have the best finds," a voice boomed from the doorway. Andie turned to see a woman in a wheelchair. She had curly gray hair and looked to be ninety if she was a day.

"Oh, Sheila, this is my sister Bridget," Addie said. Addie often thought Andie was her younger sister Bridget, so the mis-introduction didn't bother Andie much.

Apparently it didn't bother the woman either. She winked at Andie then wheeled into the room and extended her hand. "Rita Duvalle."

"Andie Miller." Andie shook her hand then lowered her voice. "Addie's daughter."

Rita smiled and nodded. "I live here at Tall Pines in the independent living section. I like to come over to the memory care unit and help out with the activities. My body might not work so good anymore, but the brain needs to stay active." She tapped the side of her head with a gnarled finger.

"Rita is very good at painting too," Addie said, glancing at the paint-splotched paper hanging on her wall. It was one of Addie's creations, which she was very proud of.

"Sorry to barge in," Rita said. "But I couldn't help but overhear you mentioning antiques. I was an antique dealer my whole life. Miss all that old stuff. It has a way of getting into your blood, doesn't it?"

"It sure does." Andie was enjoying helping with Tides, but she had to admit the pull to get back to her world of dusty old pieces of furniture and long-forgotten family heirlooms was strong. "I work at Christies as an appraiser."

Rita's brow shot up. "Oh, how interesting. I thought about going that route but found that setting up shop here in town was much more interesting."

Andie was intrigued. "Really? How so?"

Rita tilted her head as she considered the question. "I guess you'd say it's the people. The connection to the families. The opportunity for undiscovered finds."

"Undiscovered finds? I wouldn't think there would be much of that in a small town."

"You'd be surprised. There's actually a better chance. These frugal New Englanders never throw anything out, and unlike in the big city, it's not all picked over."

"I guess you have a point there." Most of the collections that Andie appraised had been carefully curated, and there weren't many surprises to be found. Could Rita be on to something? But there was no big auction house around Lobster Bay.

"But the thing I liked the most is the stories. People would come into my shop and ask me to hoe out their attic. Every item had a personal story. You wouldn't believe some of the things I found! Civil War papers, old diaries. It's so rewarding to connect with the actual ancestors of the people who owned the items."

"So you had a shop here in town?" Andie didn't remember any antique shop, but then she hadn't really paid much attention to what was in town for the past thirty years.

"Still do, actually. Oh, I can't run it anymore." Rita gestured to the wheelchair. "Body's too old to get around, but I couldn't bear to sell it. I own the building. Antique store downstairs, apartment upstairs. There's still quite a bit of inventory in the store."

"See, now you can follow your passion and stay here and help Daddy and me with Tides," Addie said matter-of-factly. Even though she was mixed up on who was here running Tides, the sentiment was the same.

It got Andie wondering... would she be as happy here running an antique store as she was as an appraiser at one of the best auction houses in the world? Then again, was she really happy in her current job? "Civil War papers and old diaries are interesting, and I like dealing with the people, but I'm sure there's nothing of real significance in these old towns."

Rita shook her head. "Not true. Old Harry Westin came in with a tiny painting he found in his mother's jewelry box, and it turned out to be an old Russian icon dating to the 1300s. How it got in Harry's mother's jewelry box is a mystery, but it was quite a find, as it was in incredibly good condition. Written up in all the papers."

Andie thought she remembered something about that.

"And don't forget, we have one of the oldest houses in New England right here in town, and it's just bursting with undiscovered treasures." Rita's eyes lit up.

"The Thompson house." Andie had heard rumors about the house, one even claiming that it had been part of the Underground Railroad and another that it had been a hideout of Blackbeard the pirate. She didn't think either of them were true, but the house was still interesting because of its age.

"Thompson?" Addie cut in, her face drawn in a scowl. "Did you say Sadie Thompson? I wouldn't trust anything she has. She stole my green sweater!"

"Oh dear. That was probably just an honest mistake, don't you think?" Rita said to Addie.

Addie's scowl deepened. "No."

Rita turned to Andie. "It happens a lot here. People forget which items are theirs."

"I can imagine." Andie remembered the sweater incident well. They actually had found her mother's sweater in Sadie's room. "Sadie is here at Tall Pines."

"Yes, I know. Her room is right down the hall. I never did talk her into letting me into the attic. The house has been in the same family for three hundred years. Oh, the things that might be there! But I guess it won't happen now. Don't know why I'm holding on to that shop. Won't be of use to me. I suppose I should think of selling, but it would have to be to the right person." Rita raised a brow and looked at Andie out of the corner of her eye then clapped her hands. "Well, I suppose I better get going. I wanted to help with the sing-along. You coming, Addie?"

Addie jumped up. "Oh yes! I'll go with you. Bye, Bridgie."

As Andie watched them leave, she felt something shift in her perspective. Was she ready to give up her dream career at Christies and start a new one in Lobster Bay?

✿

Andie took the long way out of Tall Pines so she could peek into Sadie Thompson's room.

The old woman must not have liked sing-alongs,

65

because she was sitting in a recliner, the television remote in her weathered hand, as the TV blared a talk show. She might be missing her memories, but she was alert. Her head swiveled to the door, her forehead creasing. "Addie?"

"It's Andie, actually, Addie's daughter." The similar names were confusing enough, but Andie did look like her mother.

"Don't you fool with me. I know who you are. Are you going to the dance tonight? I heard Bobby Gleason will be there." Sadie looked quite pleased about this.

Andie didn't know who Bobby Gleason was, but it was clear that Sadie thought she was a teen again. Sadie and Addie used to hang around back then. Andie was used to these fuzzy memories from her mother. She and Jane had decided it was better to play into the memories as long as they were pleasant. Trying to remind Addie of the year or to get her to recognize who someone really was only brought confusion and anger.

Andie stepped into the room. "Of course I'm going. It should be fun."

Sadie nodded, her eyes clouding for a second then clearing again. "You can come over before the dance if you want."

"That sounds nice. I've always liked your house. It's so old and charming."

Sadie nodded, her face lighting up. "Built by my granddaddy's granddaddy's granddaddy."

"I bet there are a lot of memories in there." Andie wasn't prying, not really. Sadie seemed so happy to be talking about the house that Andie couldn't help but encourage her to get lost in those memories. Who knew how long she'd have those for?

"Oh yes. And there's a library and a conservatory and secret passages."

"Secret passages?" Andie's thoughts went to the rumors. "Have you been in them?"

Sadie laughed. "Of course, silly. Remember we went in one together? But we didn't go up in the attic. Mom said there was too much junk up there."

"Excuse me. Just *who* are you?"

The angry voice made Andie whirl around, guilt heavy in her stomach. Not that she'd been doing anything wrong, but the way the woman was looking at her, you'd have thought she'd been torturing the poor old lady.

The woman in the doorway was about Andie's age. She was short and wide, her auburn hair fell to her shoulders, and her emerald-green eyes brimmed with suspicion.

Andie stuck her hand out. "I'm Andie Miller. My mom, Addie, is a resident here. She used to be friends with Sadie."

The woman glanced at Andie's hand as if it were poison. "So you know my mother?"

Andie let her hand drop. "Well, not technically, but..."

"Then why are you here talking about our house? Are you one of those opportunists trying to buy the place for cheap? I've had enough of that." The woman brushed past Andie to her mother's side. "Are you okay, Mom?"

"Of course, Emily. I was just chatting with Addie. You remember Addie."

Emily glared over at Andie. "I think *Addie* was just going."

"Right." Andie smiled at Sadie. "Nice talking to you."

She turned and left Emily to cluck over her mother. Apparently she wouldn't be making friends with Sadie's daughter anytime soon.

CHAPTER SIX

*J*ames was miserable without Maxi. He'd picked up the phone at least a dozen times to call her, but he didn't want to push her away more. Hopefully she just needed a little break and would come back soon.

He was starting to realize how much she did around the house. It had only been two days, but the sink was already full of dirty dishes, and his clothes needed to be laundered. First he'd have to figure out how to run the washing machine. And who knew how often a litter box needed to be emptied? Yech!

Coming home from work to an empty house was the pits, he thought as he slid his key into the lock. He opened the door with none of his usual enthusiasm as he clawed at his tie and stepped inside.

What in the world—

The house hadn't been in its usual neat array now with Maxi gone, but this took the cake. Something—toilet paper, he thought—had been spooled around the living room, over the chair and around the couch, and sitting at the end of it was Picasso.

"What have you done?"

Mew!

Picasso ran off to the kitchen and lurked around his food bowl while James followed the toilet-paper path to the bathroom, where almost a whole roll of it had been spooled off with Picasso's needle-like claws.

He was starting to regret adopting Picasso, especially since the main reason for it—Maxi—didn't even know about him.

Not wanting to get his suit dirty, he went upstairs to change. Picasso followed, batting at the leg of his pants as he walked up the stairs. Great, now he'd have little holes in the hemline.

He put his suit away and spent another five minutes trying to shoo Picasso out of the closet. The cat finally got the message and retreated to the bed, which he climbed up on by using his claws on the silk bed skirt. He then proceeded to glare at James as he rummaged through the bureau for jeans and a T-shirt.

James didn't dare open the sweater drawer. Picasso had developed a crush on his cashmere sweater vest, and anytime he opened that drawer, the cat would jump in and start kneading it. That sweater was expensive!

"Now I know why they make kittens so cute. You'd want to strangle them otherwise."

Picasso followed him downstairs and perched atop a bookcase, glaring down in superiority as James cleaned up the mess.

"I guess I should have appreciated Maxi more." James glanced up at the cat. Did he just nod in agreement? "I will when she gets back."

Mew.

"Good question. Where is she? Probably with Claire or Jane." James glanced at the phone he'd tossed on the table. "At least she answers my texts so I know she's safe."

He'd thought Maxi would have been back by now. She must be really mad about something, but James had sensed more than anger in her when she'd left that night. She'd seemed hurt and maybe a bit disappointed. For the life of him, he couldn't think of what he had done to make her feel that way.

With the toilet paper all gathered in a pile and stuffed in a trash bag, he glanced into the bathroom, wondering if he should take the toilet paper roll out of the holder and put it out of reach. "Maxi would know exactly what to do. She knows what to do about everything."

Picasso glared down at him in reproachful silence.

"Oh, I see, you think it's my fault she left." Was it? Of course it must have been. "All right, then, I guess there is only one thing left to do. If it's something I've done, then there must be a way to undo it. We need to figure out exactly what action I have to take to get her back."

CHAPTER SEVEN

*M*axi fiddled nervously with her coffee cup and studied the man across the table from her, Chandler Vanbeck. They were sitting in the Townline Diner, a retro-style eatery that was decorated with a lot chrome and Naugahyde. They made good coffee, and it seemed like a neutral place to meet, which was why Maxi had suggested it.

Chandler had just finished updating her on the renovation efforts in the building on the edge of Perkins Cove that he'd secured for his art gallery.

"I know it's an aggressive schedule, but I want to have the gallery open by Thursday, and I'd love to feature some of your work," Chandler said.

Maxi was taken aback. Chandler seemed like a nice guy. And he certainly seemed interested in her work, if not maybe a little *too* interested. Maxi wondered vaguely if he was interested in more than just her work. The thought was awkward and unappealing. She had no intention of having a relationship with anyone. The mere thought of it made her feel resistant and sad because deep down, she still loved James.

"But I've never shown my work anywhere. I haven't even finished a proper painting in decades." Maxi thought about the seascape she'd started the other day. It was sitting on the easel at her cottage, the paint still wet.

"It's fine," Chandler assured her. "I like to highlight emerging local artists, and no one expects them to have a following."

"I'm hardly emerging."

"You could be if you put some work in the show. Just three pieces."

Maxi sipped her coffee and contemplated Chandler's offer. Could she even get three pieces done by then? But she sensed that this was a once-in-a-lifetime chance. If she passed it up now, she might not get an offer again. "Okay, I'll do it."

"Wonderful!" Chandler stuck his hand across the table, and Maxi shook it. "I'll need the paintings by Wednesday afternoon. Will that work?"

A wave of panic struck Maxi, but she managed to nod. "Yes, that will be fine."

"Chandler! I thought I might find you here." A woman who Maxi judged to be in her early seventies stood at the end of their table. She had close-cropped white hair and bright-red-framed glasses, and was wearing a colorful flowing skirt and dozens of bangles. She looked artsy and airy and like everything Maxi was hoping to become. She smiled at Maxi and stuck her hand out. "Hi. I'm Muriel Fox."

Maxi shook her hand, feeling suddenly out of place in her crisp white blouse and tan Bermuda shorts. "Maxi Stevens."

"Nice to meet ya, Maxi." The woman turned to Chandler. "Are you going to be at the Purple Blueberry later on? Gerry is going to recite some of his poetry."

Chandler smiled. "I wouldn't miss it."

"Okay, see you then." She smiled at Maxi then turned and walked back to the counter, where a cup of coffee and piece of pie awaited.

"Have you been to the Purple Blueberry?" Chandler asked.

"I've heard of it, never been." The Purple Blueberry was a trendy little outdoor bar where the more artsy crowd hung out. Maxi had always been curious but never brave enough to go. James thought anything artsy was too "Bohemian" for someone like a bank president —or his wife—to be seen at. She was sure Claire or Jane would have gone with her, but she'd never considered asking them because she didn't want James to be mad. She didn't have to worry about what he would think anymore, but that was bittersweet.

"If you'd like to go this afternoon, I'll be going around five," Chandler said.

Warning bells surfaced. Was that just a friendly invitation or a date? Either way, best for Maxi not to encourage too much friendship from Chandler. She didn't want to send the wrong message.

"Thanks, but I can't. I have plans with Jane and Claire." At least she didn't have to lie. They were meeting at Splash at five.

Maxi couldn't wait to meet Jane and Claire and tell them the exciting news about the art gallery. As she sipped her coffee, a smile spread across her face. She was finally on her way to having everything she always wanted. Well, everything except James.

CHAPTER EIGHT

"So you haven't gone back home?" Jane asked as the waitress slid pink frothy drinks with pineapple slices perched on the rims in front of them. They were seated at Splash, one of their favorite gathering spots. It was a bar right on the beach and had all the sights, sounds, and smells of the ocean. The beachgoers had packed up their things and left, but the coconut scent of suntan lotion still lingered in the air. They could hear the lulling sound of the waves, and the colorful blues and pinks of the sun setting behind them completed the picture.

"No chance of that." Maxi actually hadn't even considered it. Sure, she felt a little homesick, and when she thought about James, her heart felt like it was broken into a million pieces, but she was determined to focus on the positive.

She loved having her own place and loved the beach, and Rembrandt was turning out to be a great addition to her life. Since moving to the cottage, she'd spent most of her time painting and had enjoyed every minute of it. Why hadn't she done this sooner? Not leaving James—she never would have done that if it hadn't been for the cheating—but getting a space of her own to pursue her creative endeavors was something she should have done years ago.

"Are you sure?" Claire picked a sweet potato fry out of the basket and dipped it in the horseradish sauce. "You and James have been together for a long time. Maybe you're just having a rough patch."

Maxi sighed and reached into her tote bag for the card. She knew she'd have to tell Claire and Jane sooner or later, but something felt wrong about the situation. It almost felt as if *she* were betraying James and not the other way around.

"It's not just a rough patch. I found this in his pocket." She held the card up. Jane and Claire both looked confused.

Claire reached for the card and put it on the table in front of her. "Sandee's business card?"

"Except I don't think James had it for business." Maxi reached out and flipped the card over. "Looks like her personal number is on the back."

Claire pressed her lips together. "It could be. I don't know her number."

78

"I figure her work number is the one actually printed on it, but this is seven digits. So it's probably a personal number she gives out to a select few." Maxi turned to Jane. "Remember when you thought you saw James with Sandee at the cottage?"

Jane nodded solemnly. "But you said you weren't in the market to buy one."

"Right. I don't think James was there looking at real estate... if you know what I mean."

"There could be a logical explanation—" Jane started, but Maxi cut her off.

"That's what I hoped at first. But then I thought about all the nights he came home late and how things have been strained between us. The real kicker was the other day when I saw him pulling out of the spot next to the real estate office, and he pretended that he didn't even see me!"

Claire's eyes narrowed. "And you think he was visiting Sandee. In broad daylight? That would be just like her. She's a home-wrecker with no conscience."

Maxi knew very well what Sandee was capable of. She'd lived through it with Claire when Claire's husband, Peter, had cheated on her with Sandee. And now it was happening to her. But it had worked out good for Claire. She'd eventually been able to start Sandcastles and now had everything she'd ever wanted, including a new devoted boyfriend. In a way, it had inspired Maxi because she knew that she, too, could use this as a way to reinvent herself into everything she always wanted to be. Just without the boyfriend.

"And he admitted to seeing her?" Jane's tone was skeptical.

"No, not really. But when I confronted him about pretending not to see me in the street, he lied and said he wasn't there!" Maxi took a long sip of her drink. "I know him well enough to know when he's lying."

"I can't believe it." Jane's expression softened with sympathy. "You always seemed so good together. What can I do to help?"

Maxi shook her head. "Nothing. I'm doing fine, really."

"You are?" Claire studied her. "Sometimes it doesn't hit you for a while. If you need to talk, please let me know. I've been there."

Maxi appreciated her friends' offers to help, but she was surprised to find that she really was doing okay. "I'm just focusing on the future. I love the little cottage. I've been painting and... I have a new man in my life."

Claire and Jane were taken aback. "So soon?"

Maxi pulled her phone out of her tote. She'd taken several pictures of Rembrandt to show them. She'd yet to tell them about the cat and was excited to surprise them. She thumbed through for her favorite, the one in which he was reaching up with one paw at her.

"His name is Rembrandt."

Claire and Jane tilted their heads to look at the phone.

"How adorable!"

"How old is he?"

"He's only six months." Maxi's heart swelled as she swiped to the next photo of him curled up and sleeping on the couch.

"Already spoiled, I see," Claire said.

"He's great company. And the cottage is coming around." Maxi took her phone back. "Do you guys want to come over and meet him and see the place tomorrow night?"

"Of course!" Jane said.

"That would be perfect," Claire agreed.

"Good. I might be really busy the next couple of days." Despite the grim news about her marriage, Maxi was bubbling over to tell her best friends about her show in the art gallery.

"Oh? Why is that?" Jane asked around a mouth of fries.

"I'm going to be showing three paintings in Chandler Vanbeck's new art gallery."

Claire's and Jane's eyes grew wide.

Jane clapped her hands. "That's wonderful!"

"Congratulations! I'm so excited for you!" Claire held up her drink, and they all clinked glasses.

Maxi took a deep breath. "I'm not going to lie, I'm

terrified. But I met with Chandler Vanbeck, and I figured if I turned him down, he might not offer again so..."

"You'll do great," Jane assured.

"Well, I don't have time to dwell on it because he wants three paintings, and I only have a couple of days to get them done."

"Oh, I guess you *will* be busy."

"I think that will be good. I feel like this is a new chance for me to do all the things I never did when I was busy raising the kids and being a model wife." Maxi made a face. "All the things that James didn't seem to approve of."

"Good for you. I know it hurts now, but look at me. Peter hooking up with Sandee was really for the best." Claire glanced around the restaurant then lowered her voice. "And I can't say it does feel like just deserts that Sandee is cheating on Peter. He deserves it."

"Payback is a bitch." Jane bit into the pineapple from her drink.

"Yeah, he deserves it." Maxi's look turned serious. "But don't let that poison you about all guys. Your two seem to be real gems."

Both Claire and Jane blushed.

"Let's hope so. I'm taking things slow," Jane said.

"Me too," Claire agreed. "Actually, I think our two guys are over at Salty's watching the ball game together."

Jane's left brow quirked up. "Oh? Good for them. I wouldn't want them to get too dependent on hanging out with us. We girls need our space."

"Here, here." Maxi raised her glass, and they all clinked again.

ames's hunch that Maxi might be at Splash with Jane and Claire turned out to be correct. She looked happy, laughing and talking and sipping one of those frou-frou drinks she liked. She looked good, too, in one of those shirts with the wide loose sleeves that she sometimes wore.

He loved seeing her happy, but this time, it broke his heart because she wasn't happy with *him*. When was the last time they'd laughed together like that?

He stood in the shadows on the beach where he could see the patio, but no one could see him. He felt like a creepy stalker, but he wasn't stalking Maxi, not really. It was just that he'd been so desperate to see if she was okay that he'd taken to scoping out the places that she liked to frequent.

But now that he'd seen her, he knew he should

leave. He turned, causing an avalanche of sand to fall into his Italian leather loafers. Darn it! Those things cost a bundle and were shined to perfection. He bent down to brush them off, taking care of a few white hairs Picasso had managed to deposit on the cuff of his slacks in the process.

He probably shouldn't have worn his good slacks and shoes to the beach, but James prided himself on his appearance. That was one thing he and Maxi had in common... they always dressed properly.

Except...

He glanced back over at the patio. Maxi wasn't wearing one of her usual muted-toned tailored outfits but was wearing something colorful and loose. She usually dressed in a more business-like manner. He'd complimented her on that many times, telling her she looked classy. But he'd noticed whenever he traveled, she took to wearing the more bohemian-style outfits... was that because of his influence? He liked those outfits, too, but he'd never complimented her on them.

Now that he thought back, Maxi had tried to encourage him to dress down a bit. Like he used to when they were younger, she'd said. Was that one of the reasons she was unhappy with him? He had been less conservative in their younger days, but once he started moving up in the bank, he had more responsibility and had to keep up appearances. He couldn't act or dress like a carefree youth anymore. Had he gone too far?

Walking in the dark back to the parking lot, James wondered if it wasn't time to make a change. Looking around, he noticed the other people walking in and out of the shops had on T-shirts and shorts. No one was dressed for success. He looked out of place.

Maybe it was time for a change. Maybe it was time to loosen up a bit about his reputation and how things looked.

James headed up the street toward a crowded tavern he'd seen a few streets over. He was going to do something he hardly ever did anymore. He was going to a bar for a beer.

"Yes!" Mike Henderson fist-bumped Rob Bradford as the Red Sox scored a triple homer. They were playing against the Yankees, and everyone in Salty's was jazzed that they were winning.

Mike didn't know Rob well, but he liked him. He seemed like a stand-up guy, and Jane had said he'd helped her a lot with her mother. That was good enough for him.

"Hey, is that Maxi's husband over there?" Rob nodded his chin toward the door.

Mike squinted through the crowd. He'd only met Maxi's husband, James, a couple of times in passing, but it did look like the guy. "I think so."

"Looks like he just got out of a boardroom meeting," Rob said. "Should we invite him to join us?"

"Sure. Maxi, Jane, and Claire are all together, so we might as well be too." Mike turned and waved at James. The guy really did look like he'd come from a board meeting with his linen slacks and polo shirt, quite a contrast to Mike's black T-shirt and tan board shorts.

It took a second for James to recognize Mike and figure out that he was waving him over. They shook hands all around, and then James pulled a barstool up to the pub table they were sitting at and ordered a Sam Adams Boston Lager.

"So, you looking for something to do while Maxi is out with Jane and Claire?" Rob asked.

James glanced from Rob to Mike. "I... I guess you could say that."

Mike could sense something was off. "They're at Splash, aren't they?"

"Yeah, it's just..." James let his voice trail off and looked down into his beer.

"Is something wrong?" Rob must have picked up on the vibe too.

James sighed. "It's just that Maxi and I aren't together anymore. I would have thought you guys knew that from Jane and Claire."

"What? No." Rob looked at Mike.

Mike shrugged and shook his head. Jane hadn't mentioned anything, but this didn't seem like something she would talk lightly about. Maxi and James had been married a long time. They had kids. This was serious.

"What happened?" Mike asked.

James shrugged. "I wish I knew. I came home the other day, and she had her bags packed."

"With no warning?" Rob looked skeptical.

James grimaced. "Well, now that I look back, I could see she was bored after the kids left. I encouraged her to take up painting. Thought that would be enough, but I guess not."

"Darn, tough break." Rob swigged his beer, his eyes drifting back to the television.

"I just can't figure it out." James sounded downright despondent. "I wish I knew why she was so mad. I'd try to rectify it if I knew what to do."

Mike shrugged. "Who knows what women want? Sometimes they're hard to figure out." Like Mike's last girlfriend, Tiffany. She'd kept him on his toes by saying one thing but then doing the opposite. And no one should even get him started on how she refused to accept that they were broken up, even though he'd explained it to her face-to-face and in the nicest way possible. Maybe he'd been too nice about it? Even now, he felt a pang of dread when he looked at his phone, thinking it might be her with another text expecting them to get back together.

Thankfully, Jane wasn't like that. At least she didn't seem to be. It might have been because Tiffany had been a lot younger than Mike, and Jane was eight years older, or maybe it was just that their relationship was so new that she was on her best behavior. Either way, Mike had already discovered that Jane was a lot more mature.

"So I guess Jane or Claire didn't say anything about why Maxi left?" James had a pleading look in his eye that reminded Mike of how Cooper looked when he wanted some table scraps.

"No. Sorry." Rob did sound genuinely sorry.

James took a pull of his beer. "I just wish I knew what to do to get her back. I don't want to push her—I get that she probably needs some space. I thought she'd come back after a night away, but it's been a couple of days now, and I don't think she is. I'm clueless as to what to do to get her back."

The poor guy was miserable. Too bad Mike had no idea how to help him. But he knew a few people that might. "If you really want to know what to do to get Maxi back, then I think you need to talk to Jane and Claire."

CHAPTER TEN

"**M**axi really seems to be doing well," Jane said the next morning as she stood outside Sandcastles, talking to Claire. She was waiting to meet Mike so they could take Cooper for a walk on the beach then head to Tall Pines to visit her mother and his grandfather.

"Yeah, almost *too* well." Claire handed Jane a white bakery bag. Inside were two chocolate chip muffins, Addie's favorites. "Take these to your mom."

"Thanks." Jane opened the bag, stuck her nose in, and closed her eyes as she inhaled. "Smells delicious. Anyway, I hope Maxi can keep her spirits up. She certainly is keeping busy with the paintings for the art show, and she also volunteered to paint the candles for the wedding."

"That art show is going to be really good for her."

Claire bent to pet Cooper, who had been obediently sitting next to Jane, watching their conversation. "How is the wedding going?"

Jane rolled her eyes. "I can't wait until it's over. I'm thinking about putting Andie in charge of guest check-in."

Claire's left brow quirked up. "Oh? So does that mean Andie is staying?"

"She hasn't said as much, but she also hasn't said anything about leaving either." Jane didn't want to get her hopes up, but she really did want her sister to stay. She'd seen her in a different light over the past two weeks, and they'd bridged some of the gap that had happened in their relationship over the last few decades.

Claire's eyes drifted over Jane's shoulder, and her face immediately lit in a smile. Jane didn't have to turn around to know that Rob Bradford was coming from his store across the street.

"Hey, Jane, how are you?" Rob came to stand beside Claire, his smile matching hers.

"Good. You? How's the bread biz?"

"Great. Gaining business every day." Rob looked over at his store with pride. "I love being here in Lobster Bay. In fact, last night Mike and I had a great time at Salty's. Ran into Maxi's husband there." Rob's expression turned serious. "I didn't realize they were having trouble."

Jane's warm feelings were replaced by anger for James. "Yeah, turned out he's not such a great guy."

"After all those years of marriage. We've known him as long as Maxi, and I've always liked him, even though he's a bit stuffy," Claire said. "But I never expected he was a cheater."

"A cheater?" Rob frowned at Claire. "What do you mean?"

Claire glanced around to make sure they couldn't be overheard. "Yes, he cheated on Maxi. That's why she left."

Rob made a face. "Are you sure? Because the guy I talked to last night didn't seem like a cheater. In fact, he seemed oblivious to the reasons why Maxi left."

"Huh? That can't be right."

Cooper let out a small bark, and his tail started thumping. Jane turned to see Mike coming up the street. As he joined the group, he took Cooper's leash, his hand brushing Jane's and causing her heart to flutter.

"Hey, Mike." Rob and Mike shook hands. "Didn't you think James seemed sincerely baffled as to why Maxi left when we talked to him last night?"

"Yeah, the guy was practically crying."

"Claire and Jane said that Maxi thinks he cheated," Rob said.

"Cheated? No. He wants her back. Did she talk to him about the cheating? Because he didn't mention that. He seemed genuinely in the dark about what was bothering her. I think he'd know what it was if he was cheating on her." Mike bent down to rub Cooper's neck.

Claire pressed her lips together. "Well, I don't think she mentioned it exactly, but he's been acting funny, and she found a card with a phone number."

"Is it possible this is just a miscommunication?" Rob asked.

Claire shook her head. "I don't think so. There were other signs."

Rob shrugged. "I don't know. If you saw how James was last night, the last thing I would suspect would be that he had another woman. If he did, why would he seem so clueless about why Maxi left and desperate to get her back?"

Claire put her hands on her hips and looked up at Rob. "You're too nice to notice, but cheaters always lie. I know from experience. I bet if I talked to him, I'd pick up the lie in a heartbeat."

"Good, because you're going to get that chance."

"I am?" Claire asked.

Mike nodded. "Yep, last night we advised James that if he wanted to get Maxi back, you and Jane were the ones to talk to."

❦

Maxi glanced at the ocean then back at her painting. She leaned in, dabbing a line of bright-white paint along the top of the wave. She wanted her painting to be realistic, to capture the way it actually looked when the sun hit the foamy crest of the wave. She glanced back at the ocean. Not too bad.

She'd been working for several hours, and this one was almost done. One down, two to go. But if she could finish them as quickly as this one, she'd have no problem making the deadline for the art show.

Putting her brush in a bottle of turpentine, she stretched and flexed her fingers. Her hand was slightly cramped from holding the brush for so long, but it was surprising how quickly she got back into the rhythm of painting after not having done it for so long. The soothing cadence of the waves and the sea air helped.

A noise drew her attention toward the cottage. Rembrandt sat on the back of the couch, looking out the window. He raised his paw and tapped on the glass, his adorable big eyes looking right at her. Her heart swelled. Adopting the cat definitely had been the right thing to do. He was good company, and she barely even missed James. Of course, that could be because James hadn't been home much for the past few months anyway, so there wasn't much to miss.

She took her paints and dirty brushes and turpentine inside. Time for a break. As soon as she got in, Rembrandt scampered over to her. She picked him up and cuddled him under her chin, looking back out at the beach.

Over by the shoreline, a golden dog ran past. Cooper? Must have been because Jane and Mike followed, holding hands and laughing. Maxi was happy that Jane had finally found someone. She could have gone out to say hi, but they looked so involved in each other that she didn't want to interrupt them.

Maxi cherished her good friends, but now that her life was changing, maybe it was time to make some different friends. She put Rembrandt on the chair and picked up the local paper. Hadn't she seen a list of events in the paper? She flipped through, finding the small section listing the events. The Purple Blueberry was having a wine tasting tomorrow afternoon. That might be fun to go to. Did she dare?

She grabbed the charcoal pencil from the coffee table and circled the ad then folded the paper and put it on the table so she could find it later. She'd better get busy. She had to clean the place up and had a few pieces of artwork to hang and some throw rugs to put down. She wanted the place to look as good as it could for Jane and Claire tonight.

🍀

Mike wouldn't have thought it possible, but his grandfather had improved since he'd been at Tall Pines. At first he'd been afraid that taking Gramps out of the home he'd known for forty years would make him deteriorate even faster, but it hadn't. Instead he'd thrived with the care and people to socialize with.

The frequent visits from Cooper and Mike seemed to perk him up even more. Another reason for Mike to give up his apartment in Seattle and stay in Lobster Bay.

"Now you be a good boy." Gramps smiled down at Cooper. The dog was still damp from his romp on the beach, but that didn't stop Gramps from petting the dog's fur. If dogs could smile, Cooper would have been smiling right back at the old man. Gramps looked up at Mike. "Looks like you're taking him for lots of walks on the beach. He loves that."

"He's getting good care," Mike said. Even though Cooper was now living with Jane because Mike couldn't have him at the cottage he was renting, he still spent a lot of time with the dog, which had the happy consequence that he also spent a lot of time with Jane.

"Jane sure has been spoiling him. Looks like maybe she's been taking good care of you too." Gramps sat back in his chair, sparkling blue eyes assessing Mike and making him a little uncomfortable.

"She's a good friend."

Gramps laughed. "Come on now, I think there's more than that."

Mike smiled. "Maybe. There's no reason to rush things."

Gramps eyed him. "Sure, just don't let her get away."

"Don't worry, I don't plan to." Which was really his main reason to stay in Lobster Bay. Mike had never met anyone like Jane. She was sweet and pretty and mature. And even though their relationship was still new, he knew in his gut that she was the one. But Jane seemed a little more cautious, and Mike was taking things slow. Couldn't blame her—she'd been widowed and hadn't dated in decades. She was easing into the relationship, and Mike didn't want to rush and scare her off.

"Speaking of which, she's probably ready to leave." Mike patted his leg, and Cooper nudged Gramps's hand for one last pet then trotted to his side. "See you tomorrow."

Out in the hall, Mike's phone rang. It was Tim, his buddy from Seattle. He paused in front of the door to the memory care wing, where Jane was visiting her mother.

"Hey, Tim, how's it going?"

"Great. How about you? Beach life must suit you, since you haven't come back yet."

Mike laughed. "I guess it does."

"And your grandfather?"

"He's doing really good."

"Great! Hey, I found someone who wants to sublet your apartment, so if you're really serious about staying out there, maybe you can switch over the lease."

Initially Mike had come to Lobster Bay just to get his grandfather settled. He'd intended to return to

Seattle and had been paying a lot of money to keep his apartment there. But that was before he met Jane. "I am serious about staying."

"Okay. I'll send you the contact info. Gonna miss you back here. And I'm not the only one." Tim's pause made Mike feel uneasy. "There's some other news too."

"Oh?" Mike looked down at Cooper, who was looking up at him, his brow slightly wrinkled as if he sensed Mike's concern.

"Tiffany is apparently taking a trip to Lobster Bay."

"What? Aww, come on! Does she still think we are getting back together?" He could not have been clearer to her that their relationship was over. Should he have been more forceful? Maybe he should have yelled instead of calmly discussing it with her. The girl did seem to thrive on drama.

"She said she's going there for some art gallery opening, but of course she was asking if you were still out there."

Darn! The last thing Mike wanted was Tiffany hanging around trying to get back together. But there really was a new art gallery opening up—Maxi was showing some paintings at the opening. Was it possible that Tiffany really was coming out for that and not to get back together? She hadn't messaged him since a few weeks ago when he'd had to make it brutally clear. It was possible she was asking if he was still there so she could *avoid* him. Wishful thinking, perhaps?

Thoughts of the gallery made him think about Maxi and James. Mike made a mental note to try to persuade Jane to talk to James. He had a feeling the guy was sincere and totally lost without his wife.

He hung up with Tim just as Jane was coming out the door.

"Something wrong?" Her blue eyes were dark with concern as they flicked to the phone in his hand.

Mike took her hand. "Of course not. That was Tim. I might have someone to take over my lease in Seattle."

Jane smiled. "Really? So you really are going to stay?"

"I think so. There's a lot of benefits to staying in Lobster Bay."

Jane nodded and stepped past him to lead the way down the hall.

"Good, Cooper will be happy about that," she teased over her shoulder.

Mike fell in step with her. "Hey, speaking of happy... I was wondering if you wouldn't mind hearing James Stevens out."

Jane's smile faltered. "You really think I should talk to him? I know you and Rob mentioned it this morning, but I don't know if that's a good idea."

"I think you should hear him out. Honestly, the guy was hurting. I'm convinced he didn't do anything wrong and really wants her back."

Jane stopped and turned to him. "Really? Why?"

"Just a feeling. When you see the guy, you'll see what I mean." Mike put on his most sincere face.

Jane rolled her eyes. "Okay, fine. But only because you're vouching for his innocence. I still think he's a louse. But I'll talk to Claire, and if she agrees, then *maybe* we'll see what he has to say."

CHAPTER ELEVEN

"What should I wear to meet with Jane and Claire?" James glanced back at Picasso, but the cat was no help. He barely slitted an ice-blue eye at him from his position curled up on the bed.

James was regretting setting up the meeting, even though it was probably his best chance of winning Maxi back. The frigid tone in Jane's voice when he'd called made him realize that convincing them to help might be difficult. But why was she so cold toward him? Was it just that she was acting standoffish in support of Maxi? He'd done nothing wrong.

Now the thought of meeting with both Jane and Claire, who he assumed would be equally icy, terrified him.

"Clothing is important, and I want to make a favorable impression so that they can see their way toward helping me." James laid out some slacks and shirts on the bed and stood back. Slacks might be too formal. Where were his old jeans?

He pushed to the back of the closet where the clothes he hadn't worn in years still hung. One pair of jeans was all faded. That wouldn't do. He picked a stiff dark indigo pair that he'd hardly worn and brought that out to the bed.

Picasso perked up. Perhaps sensing that his white hair would make a mess on the dark blue, he stretched and wandered over to the jeans.

"Don't even think about it." James whipped the jeans off the bed and laid them on a chair. Undaunted, Picasso sat on his haunches and started to wash behind his ear.

James pulled his tie rack out of the closet and laid it on the bed. He picked out a blue paisley tie and held it up. "Maybe this one?"

Mew! Picasso swatted at the tie.

Okay, apparently he didn't like the blue tie. James held up a yellow one. "How about—"

Merow! Picasso lashed out, ripping the yellow tie from his hand and then batting all the others off the bed.

"Right. No tie. That's exactly what I was thinking." The cat might be on to something. Rob and Mike hadn't been wearing ties last night. In fact, they'd been dressed pretty casually in T-shirts and jeans. James eyed the button-down shirt he'd selected. Too formal? He didn't want Jane and Claire to feel like they were in a business meeting. Maybe it was best to dress like Mike and Rob. Did he even have any regular T-shirts?

James rummaged in the bureau, eliciting more interest from Picasso, who managed to jump on top of it so he could look down into the drawers. No doubt he was looking for the cashmere sweater vest.

The closest thing to a T-shirt was a polyester short-sleeved shirt with a pocket on the left front side. That would have to do.

James put the rest of his clothes away, got dressed, and checked himself in the mirror. He glanced over at Picasso for approval. The cat simply blinked and curled up in a ball.

"Right, not exactly the look I was going for. Maybe Jane and Claire can give me some guidance." He straightened his collar and patted the cat. It felt good to have someone to talk things over with, but Picasso was no substitute for Maxi.

Feeling like he was going to the gallows, James straightened his collar and grabbed his wallet. He glanced back at Picasso. "I'm off to see what I can do to get her back. You hold down the fort."

On the way out, James double-checked the bureau to make sure he hadn't left the cashmere sweater drawer open.

❀

"Hello, James." Jane stood with her arms crossed over her chest, trying to be polite and wondering why she'd agreed to talk to James about Maxi. If it wasn't for Mike and Rob convincing her and Claire to give James a chance, they would have turned him down outright.

"Jane, Claire. Thanks for talking to me." James cleared his throat, clearly nervous. Good. After what he'd done, he should be. But still, Jane had an inkling of a doubt about James's guilt. Mike seemed convinced that James had done nothing wrong, and if James had cheated, why would he go to the effort of arranging this meeting?

He'd clearly thought hard about it, judging by the outfit he was wearing. It looked like he was trying to be less formal. Either that, or he hadn't had a chance to do laundry since Maxi left.

"How about we go out on the back porch? It's much more scenic, and Brenda made some lemonade."

They headed out back and sat at one of the little tables. James glanced nervously at Sally, who was up on a ladder, hanging little crystal chandeliers from the ceiling. Maxi had said it would give the inn an upscale look and be perfect for weddings. At first Jane had thought they would be too fancy, but they were so small and not loaded with crystals. They gave the porch a chic look without seeming out of place.

"So what do you want?" Claire blurted out, her distaste for James obvious.

Jane poured lemonade into tall glasses while James fidgeted to come up with his answer.

"Well... I ... uh... I ran into Mike and Rob, and they said maybe you could help. I don't know what I've done to make Maxi so mad, but I want to get her back."

Jane's left brow quirked up. "You don't know what you've done?"

James looked appropriately confused. "No. Honestly. Well, okay, I know I've been working a lot, but I was trying to clear up a project so we could take a trip. Maxi always wanted to go to Italy, and I thought it would help cheer her up. And then I guess we haven't been as close as usual, but I thought maybe she was just in a funk with no kids at home. I tried to encourage her to get back into art, and then I had a few other things..."

He was rambling now, spilling it all out.

Claire cut to the chase. "And is that why you took up with Sandee Harris?"

"What? Took up?" James looked from Claire to Jane. "What do you mean?"

Claire slapped the business card she'd pocketed at Splash on the table and pointed at the number written in ink. "Why else would you have her personal number?"

James squinted. "Personal number? That's not a phone number."

Claire sat back, crossing her arms over her chest. "You can't weasel out of it that easy."

"I'm not weaseling out. That's not a phone number."

"So you deny meeting with Sandee Harris in a cottage, then?" Jane asked.

James looked sincerely baffled. "No. I did meet with Sandee. It was supposed to be a surprise."

Claire snorted. "I'll say!"

James shook his head, his face red. "It's not what you think. I was meeting with Sandee because I was looking to buy a cottage on the beach. Maxi has mentioned many times over the years that her dream is to have a little studio and paint on the beach. There aren't any commercial studio spaces on the beach, so I thought if we bought a cottage, she could use it for that."

Claire's shoulders relaxed, but her eyes were still full of suspicion. Jane couldn't blame her. She remembered that when Peter cheated, he'd been full of excuses. But this was different. "So why did you need Sandee's personal number?"

"This?" James tapped on the writing, and Claire nodded. "That's not her personal phone number. That's the price for the cottage."

Claire frowned and snatched the card up. "One million two hundred eighty-five thousand nine hundred seventy-nine." She glanced at Jane. Jane felt like an idiot. That was about the going price for small oceanfront cottages like the one she'd seen James at. Why hadn't she thought of that before?

"So you're not having any affair with Sandee?" Jane asked.

James made a face. "No. She's hardly my type. I like women that are classy. Like Maxi."

He had a point. James had always been worried about appearances, preferring Maxi to dress in conservative clothing. Sandee with her brassy blond hair, low-cut shirts, and fake boobs was hardly conservative.

Apparently Claire wasn't quite convinced. "What about when you pretended that you didn't see her downtown?"

James looked sheepish. "I panicked. That was another one of her surprises. I got her a kitten."

"You did?" Jane was incredulous. Maxi had mentioned many times that James didn't want animal hair on his suits, and he'd gotten a kitten?

"She's been acting down in the dumps lately, and I knew she wanted one." James brushed a few white hairs off his shirt and sighed. "I bought a lot of those sticky tape rollers, too, but they don't work very good."

Jane glanced at Claire. Her expression was a mix of skepticism and dawning realization that there had been a big misunderstanding. Had they misjudged James? He looked so lost and forlorn and eager for them to believe him. He'd adopted a kitten, for crying out loud! He'd clearly been very nervous coming here. A man who had been cheating wouldn't bother to put himself in that position. She'd made a big mistake, and now she needed to make up for it.

"We're seeing Maxi tonight. We'll talk to her," Jane said.

James's tight expression dissolved with relief. "I'd really appreciate that."

"She's not gonna just go back that easy," Sally piped in from atop the ladder.

James frowned and turned in his chair. "But if she left because she thought I was cheating..."

"Yeah, I know." Sally descended the ladder. "But now she's doing things she couldn't do before. She's got a little freedom. And she's probably gonna feel silly for thinking that of you. You might meet a little resistance."

"But surely she won't be mad still. Maxi is quite reasonable, and I know she loves James," Jane said.

"I know. But I have an idea. One that could work out better in the long run. I should know. I've seen this happen with lots of couples once they get to empty-nester age. They grow apart. But if you play this right, you could bring the two of you back together and solidify your marriage for the long haul," Sally said.

"Seems like Maxi coming back to the house would help with that," James said.

"Ayuh. And she might do just that, but..." Sally scrutinized James's outfit with a scowl. "Then you'd fall back into your old ways. Your relationship needs a shake-up. Maxi's already changing, and now you need to follow suit."

"She might be right. Things get stale when you've been together a long time, and Maxi's been antsy for a while, I think," Claire said.

"This would be the perfect time for a new start," Jane added.

"Ayuh," Sally said. "It's the perfect opportunity. Now you don't want to push Maxi. She's likely all worked up and will tend to think you are lying if you start pushing about how you didn't cheat. You'll put her on the defensive, and you don't want that. Let Jane and Claire clear the path. They can vouch for you, and that will go a long way to her believing it."

"Okay, that sounds easy. And then what?"

Sally cocked her head to look at his outfit again and shook her head. "Then... I think you're going to need a makeover."

Andie loved taking flowers from the gardens at Tides to her mother. It was fitting, too, since her mother had been the one to foster her interest in gardening in the first place.

Today she'd picked a small bouquet of black-eyed Susans and purple cone flowers and put them in one of her grandmother's vases to bring for Addie. The flowers always cheered her mother, and it felt like she was keeping her in touch with the gardens she'd cherished so much.

"These are lovely, dear!" Addie's face lit up as she took the vase from Andie. She sniffed the flowers, closing her eyes, her smile widening. Then she examined the vase. "Don't tell Nona you are using one of her good vases. She'll scold you."

"It will be our secret." Andie wasn't worried. Nona had died decades ago.

Andie reached for the Sandcastles bakery bag on the small desk under the window. She'd seen Jane grab the bag on her way out with Mike to visit Tall Pines and figured Claire had supplied her with a few fresh muffins for Addie. Too bad the bag was empty. She was hungry and could have used one of those chocolate chip muffins.

When she'd been picking the flowers, she'd seen Jane and Claire talking to Maxi's husband on the back porch at Tides. Looked like they were in quite the conversation. Andie wondered what that was about. Maxi and James were going through a hard time. Was he trying to weasel his way back in? Andie didn't need to worry about him pulling any shenanigans, though. She'd seen Sally join the conversation, and the old woman was sharp. She wouldn't let James pull the wool over anyone's eyes, if, in fact, that was what he was doing.

A knock on the door drew Andie from her thoughts.

Standing in the doorway was a tiny woman with wispy white hair. She had a thick maroon cardigan wrapped around her despite the fact that it was summer and the air conditioning was barely on. She had an intricate silver box clutched to her chest.

"Sorry to interrupt." Her voice was timid. "Are you the girl that knows about antiques?"

The question took her by surprise. Had Rita mentioned her to the woman? "Yes, I am."

"I'm Gloria Farnsworth. I was hoping you could look at this box for me." The woman held the box out. Even from eight feet away, Andie could see it was a high-quality piece with an intricate raised design.

"Of course, come in." Andie glanced at Addie.

"Yes, please do come in." Addie gestured for Gloria to enter.

Gloria shuffled over to Andie and handed her the box. Andie dug out her reading glasses and started to inspect it. Turning it over, she saw the English silver hallmarks for pieces made in Birmingham in 1890. "It's solid silver and old."

She inspected the sides and top. It was in great condition, the raised floral decoration very intricate. The inside was lined with cobalt-blue velvet in near perfect condition with only a few spots of wear.

"It was my grandmother's. She always said it was worth a lot." Gloria sounded hopeful.

"It is a very nice piece and in good condition. I would say it has some value." Andie guessed it was worth around a thousand dollars. The silver alone was valuable, but the craftsmanship of the piece itself raised that value, and knowing the provenance added to that even more.

"More than twenty-five dollars?" Gloria asked.

"Twenty-five! Yes, I would say around a thousand."

Gloria frowned. "Are you sure? Damien Carruthers said it's only worth twenty-five, and he would give me twenty."

"Who is Damien Carruthers?" Andie already didn't like the man if he was ripping off little old ladies. But maybe he was just not very good at valuing antiques.

"He has an ad in the classifieds to appraise antiques," Gloria said.

"Well, I might get a second opinion if I were you." Andie handed the box back. "It's worth considerably more. Of course, a dealer buying it couldn't pay one thousand, but I think you could get five or six hundred."

"Really?" Gloria looked quite pleased. "I'd sell it to you for five. I was hoping to use the money to pay for my granddaughter's 4H camp this fall."

"Oh, sorry, but I don't have a shop or anything, so I'm not in the market to make purchases. Do you have someone who can take it to a shop for you?" Since Gloria appeared to be a resident at Tall Pines, Andie figured she needed assistance.

"My daughter can help me, but she said the only shop in Lobster Bay is closed."

"Maybe take it to Portland? There are some high-end shops there that might give you a good price."

"Okay, thanks so much." Gloria nodded at Addie and shuffled out into the hall.

Andie watched her leave, a smile spreading on her face. It had felt good to help the woman. She'd had a brief moment of hoping the silver box might have been one of those rare finds she'd spent her life searching for, but helping the woman get a fair price had its own rewards. If she ever ran into this Carruthers person, she was going to give him a piece of her mind.

Outside the doorway, another resident was lingering.

"Well, what did she say?" the woman asked Gloria.

"You were right. It is worth a lot more."

The woman glanced in at Andie. "Do you think she'd look at my mother's figurines?"

Andie could hardly refuse the woman. "I'd be happy to look at them."

"Oh! I see you've found her." Rita wheeled up to them and looked up at Andie. "I hope you don't mind, but I told Gloria and Mae that you were an antique expert. I told them their things are much more valuable than Damien said. That guy is a snake."

Goria flushed. "It's not that I didn't believe you, Rita, but Damien seemed so sincere."

"Yeah, he can be very persuasive, and I realize you

can't actually shop around." Rita turned to Andie. "What Lobster Bay needs is a good reputable antique dealer these folks can come to."

Rita had a point. Apparently there was a need for someone to take in antiques here in town. It wasn't as glamorous as working for a prestigious auction house, but Andie was starting to think that Lobster Bay had a lot more to offer than New York City, and her time at Christies had proven that prestige might be overrated.

CHAPTER TWELVE

axi's excitement over showing Jane
and Claire her cottage faded as soon as
her friends arrived. Something was wrong, something
they didn't want to come right out and tell her. She
could tell by the awkward way they were acting.

"This place is adorable!" Jane exclaimed as she
handed Maxi the lobster dip she'd brought.

"And Rembrandt too!" Claire picked up the kitten
and held him up to her face, smiling and cooing at him.
Rembrandt purred and acted adorable as usual.

"It's small, but so far I'm enjoying it here." She
really was. Okay, she missed James a little, but every
time her thoughts turned to him, she shoved them away.
The sooner she stopped thinking about him, the better.

"I think it's perfect, and the scenery can't be beat."

Claire nodded to the ocean view outside the sliding-glass door.

"It needs work, but since it's not mine, I'm not putting a lot of money in. I don't mind fixing a few things, though, because it belongs to Hailey's grandpa." Maxi herded them toward the small bedroom, showing them the tiny bathroom along the way. "Of course, I decorated with my own comforter, throw rugs, and some things on the wall."

"It's very cottage chic," Jane said.

"Thanks." Maxi pulled a bottle of wine out of the fridge and grabbed three glasses. "Let's go out on the patio."

Claire put Rembrandt down and picked up the plate she'd brought, which was loaded with bite-sized pieces of cake. She held the door open for Maxi and Jane, blocking Rembrandt's exit with her foot.

The patio was Maxi's favorite part of the cottage. It was made of concrete pavers and sat level with the beach. That meant the sand often encroached on the edges, but Maxi had swept it away before the girls arrived.

Claire and Jane gasped at the painting on the easel. Maxi had to admit that she'd outdone herself. The colors were vibrant, and she'd captured the light perfectly. It was still wet—acrylic paintings took a while to dry—but that wasn't why she'd left it outside. She'd wanted her friends to see it in the natural light.

Claire turned from the painting. "It's gorgeous!"

"Stunning." Jane tilted her head as she inspected it.

"Thanks. It's easier than I thought getting back into the swing of painting. This is the first one for the gallery show. I hope the other two come as easy."

They settled into the white wooden beach chairs that were arranged in a semicircle and filled their glasses. Maxi loaded a cracker with lobster dip. Jane took a piece of cake.

Maxi washed down the cracker with a sip of wine then gave her friends a pointed look. "Okay, out with it. I know you two have something on your minds."

Claire and Jane exchanged a glance, and Maxi's stomach tightened. Hopefully they weren't going to try to talk her out of living here in the cottage. She was too emotionally invested in her new life now. But they wouldn't want her to go back to a cheater. Maybe they'd found out that James was even worse than she'd thought. That he'd been cheating for years with several people. Maxi's cheeks burned with embarrassment, and she braced herself for the worst.

"James didn't cheat on you," Claire blurted out.

"Huh?" Maxi stared, stunned. That was the last thing she'd expected to hear.

"We talked to him, and he explained about the card," Jane said.

"Sure, I just bet he did. Don't tell me you guys fell for some lame lie?"

Jane leaned forward and slathered dip on a cracker. "Of course not. We were skeptical at first too. But, Maxi, if you had seen him..."

"Yeah. He's a mess," Claire said.

Maxi wasn't buying it. "What about the card I found in his pocket?"

Jane glanced at Claire, who nodded, then said, "That wasn't a phone number. It was the price."

"The price of what?"

"A cottage."

Aha! That proved he was lying. "We weren't buying a cottage."

"Not that you knew about. James was trying to surprise you." Claire leaned forward and touched Maxi's arm, her eyes brimming with sincerity. "James had noticed that you were unhappy, and he was trying to do things to make you happier. That's why he suggested you take up art again."

"And why he was working so much. He was trying to get a project done quickly so he could take you on a trip," Jane said.

Maxi's gaze flicked from Jane to Claire and back again. They wouldn't make light of James cheating, and for them to come here on his behalf... well, they must believe him.

"Seriously? I feel like a jerk now. At least I didn't accuse him of it to his face or spread it around town."

Maxi drank down the rest of her wine then refilled her glass.

"He was kind of shocked that you thought he was cheating."

Maxi's heart was flooded with guilt. "I feel so awful. Poor James. But still…" She looked around the patio, at her painting and the cottage. And Rembrandt curled up on the back of the couch. In the few days she'd been here, she'd felt like a butterfly emerging from a cocoon. She was starting a new life, and she was afraid there might not be room for James in it. "I'm not sure I want to give everything up and go back. I'm afraid."

Jane frowned. "Afraid of what?"

"Afraid that I'll lose the momentum I've made with my art. Afraid that maybe I don't really love James like I used to. Afraid that if I go back, things will go back to the way they were, and I'll regret it for the rest of my life."

To their credit, Jane and Claire didn't try to talk her into it. Maxi needed to figure this out on her own. Yes, she owed James an apology, but things hadn't been all roses between them regardless. She wasn't ready to just go back to their house and move in like nothing had happened. Not now and maybe not ever.

CHAPTER THIRTEEN

*M*axi stared at the phone in her hand. She'd called James to apologize, and he'd taken it a lot better than she'd expected. He'd been quieter than she expected, too, probably because his feelings were hurt. She felt like a heel.

"I kind of thought he'd ask me to come back," Maxi said to Rembrandt, who was on the coffee table batting at one of her charcoal pencils.

The cat looked up at her as if to ask how she felt about that. Maxi wasn't sure. Now that she realized James wasn't a cheater, her move to the cottage seemed overly drastic. But there had been something wrong with their relationship, and she was enjoying her freedom. It had only been a few days, but she wasn't the same person she'd been when she left James.

Would James still want the new Maxi? And, more

importantly, did the new Maxi want to go back to her old life?

Oh well, nothing like immersing yourself in a painting to let the subconscious work those things out. Maxi took her palette and brushes out to the patio, where the canvas for her second painting for the art gallery opening awaited. She'd already sketched in the craggy rocks, crashing waves, and one lone seagull. She took a minute to set up the paints then grabbed her palette and mixed cerulean blue with yellow ochre for the cresting wave.

It would take several hours to lay in the basics, then she'd let it dry for a while before adding the highlights tomorrow. That would be just about the right timing to visit the Purple Blueberry for that wine tasting this afternoon.

Yesterday she'd been excited to step out to the trendy bohemian bar, something she'd always wanted to do. But today her feelings were apprehensive. In thirty years of marriage, she'd hardly gone anywhere without James at her side, and suddenly it felt like she would be missing a part of her.

But the Purple Blueberry wasn't a place that James would ever want to visit. It wasn't a place where one wore neatly pressed chinos and golf shirts. But it was a place where Maxi had always thought she'd fit in.

She felt as if she were standing on the very cliff she was painting, looking down at the ocean of her future. If she went back to James, what would become of that future? All the things she wanted—to immerse herself in creativity and find new like-minded friends and activities—might be pushed out of her reach. But yet, she couldn't imagine a future without James. Now that the sting of thinking he had cheated on her had worn off, she realized she still loved him.

She didn't want to lose him, but more than that, she didn't want to lose herself.

How in the world have I let myself get talked into this? James wondered as he stood in Montgomery's Department Store, his gaze shifting between the selections of clothing Claire and Jane held up.

James hated shopping. He usually just ordered things at O'Malley's Men's Shop. They knew his measurements. He'd pick out a suit, and Ted would tailor it for him. Casual clothing was off the rack. He always bought the same thing. But Claire and Jane and that odd handywoman, Sally, had insisted he needed to change his image.

He supposed they were right. Maxi had looked more casual the last time he saw her, and Rob and Mike didn't dress up like he did. Had he become a stodgy old man as Sally had implied?

"I like this and this." He pointed at a pair of jeans

that looked old and faded and a black T-shirt with gray stitching that made it look more tailored than a regular tee.

"I'll go grab some similar items." Sally pushed off from the rack she'd been leaning against and disappeared into the store.

"So how did Maxi seem when you saw her?" James asked Jane and Claire. He'd told them about Maxi's apology call and had even earned an awkward slap on the back from Sally when he'd explained how he'd managed to not appear too eager. Sally had advised him against begging her to come back home like he'd wanted to. She seemed to think that playing hard to get was the way to go.

James wasn't into games like that, but then again, he also knew nothing about women, and since Jane and Claire both agreed with Sally, he'd reluctantly gone along. It had been the hardest thing he'd ever done, but Picasso had been there to lend him moral support. The cat must have felt sorry for him because after the call he'd even let out a few purrs, the first time ever.

Pretending to be cool, calm, and collected, as if Maxi's absence wasn't killing him, had been the most difficult thing he'd ever done.

"She did feel terrible about suspecting you." Claire held a sky-blue shirt up under his chin and glanced at Jane for approval.

"That one brings out your blue eyes," Jane said.

"She seemed like she was settling in to the cottage, but I got the impression she misses you."

"She's just having too much fun exploring her freedom," Sally piped in as she piled three more pairs of pants into James's arms.

"It's going to take her a while to adjust. She was getting all geared up to hate you," Claire said. "In the meantime, we're going to help you out so you're well positioned to win her back.

"Thanks." James looked down at the pile of clothes. "Updating my appearance is good, I guess, but I feel like I need to take some kind of action."

"Don't worry, we have that covered too." Sally pushed him toward the changing room. "See, the thing is you need to *show* Maxi that you're willing to change. To make the relationship better for her. To give her everything she needs to live her best life."

"Okay." James drew out the word. "But how do I do that? Should I write a note? Send some flowers? Call her?"

Sally shook her head and rolled her eyes. "No. You show her by *doing*. Once we find your perfect outfit, you're going to run into Maxi on her own territory and show her you can be part of her new life."

"I am?" James asked.

"Yeah, you are." Claire motioned for him to go into the dressing room. "Don't forget to come out and show us what each outfit looks like on."

James felt stupid changing outfits and parading around in front of Maxi's friends. But if it helped get her back, he'd do it. "So how am I going to run into her on *her* territory?"

"You're going to the Purple Blueberry," Jane said. "I think she's going to a wine tasting there this afternoon. I saw it circled on the paper on her coffee table last night."

James stopped halfway into the dressing room and turned to face them. "But that's a hangout for hippies." James was very careful about where he hung out. He needed to keep up appearances.

"Yes, it is, and if you want Maxi back, it's going to become a hangout for you as well."

CHAPTER FOURTEEN

Jane returned to Tides after their shopping trip with James to find Andie on the phone in the foyer.

"Yes, we'll make sure the candles are the perfect shade of blue." Andie rolled her eyes, pointed at the phone, and mouthed, "Bridezilla."

"The cake, too, yep," Andie said into the phone. "Oh, we're all invited? How lovely." Andie made a sour face, which Jane echoed. "A full table of eight."

A table of eight? Who in the world would she put at that? Claire, Rob, Andie, herself, Mike, Maxi... an idea ran through her head. She could invite James, and maybe that would be another thing that would help push him and Maxi back together.

She felt bad for James. The poor guy was making an

effort. And he'd adopted a kitten for Maxi. If that didn't spell true love, she didn't know what did. The new clothes would make a difference. James hadn't always been so stuffy either. When they'd been younger, he'd been much more casual. Like Rob and Mike.

Thoughts of Mike reminded her of the phone call he'd gotten at Tall Pines. She'd sensed that he'd gotten some disturbing news. He'd acted different afterwards but insisted nothing was wrong. It made her feel wary, and she wondered about their relationship. Things were going well, but maybe she should be more cautious. She wasn't very experienced at dating and might be reading too much into things.

"Pink roses on the arbor?" Andie was still talking to Bridezilla on the phone. "Yes, those would look lovely with the blue bridesmaids' outfits."

Jane glanced out the window toward the garden. Andie had done a great job bringing it back to life. It was bursting with a rainbow of flowers and lush green leaves and teeming with butterflies and birds. But the rosebushes beside the arbor were red. They hadn't fully climbed the trellis either. Why in the world was Andie promising pink roses?

"Yes, lovely talking to you too. Can't wait to meet in person." Andie hung up the phone.

"You handle people a lot better than I do," Jane said. "You sounded so convincing and reassuring."

Andie laughed. "Lots of practice with high-mainte-nance antique-appraisal clients."

"What about the arbor, though? The roses are red. You promised her pink."

Andie glanced out the window. "The rosebushes needed some work. I had to cut a lot back, so they aren't tall enough to climb all the way up anyway. I've been thinking about how to handle that. Maybe we could buy pink roses and weave them in? Perhaps hang some pots of those small roses. Might look pretty to have pink at the top and red at the bottom."

"That's a good idea. I think Shane has some more work to do on the arbor. Maybe he could make some-thing so that it's easy for us to weave in fresh roses?"

"Oh, maybe."

Andie looked like she was trying to pretend lack of interest, but by the way she perked up when Jane mentioned Shane's name, Jane doubted she wasn't inter-ested. She'd noticed her sister looking around the inn as if looking for someone and had guessed it was Shane. He'd been helping Sally out with all the repairs they'd been doing but had been out of town for the past few days.

Jane decided not to comment further on Shane. "You're a real asset to the inn. Honestly, I'm not good at handling people, especially when they are demanding like our bride."

"I'm happy to help. Like I said, lots of experience."

"Well, I might have to call on that help a lot over the next week. The inn is fully booked for the wedding, and it's important that everyone is happy. That money is going a long way toward keeping Mom at Tall Pines, and good reviews will bring in more business."

"Mom's doing so good there. I'll do my best to make sure the guests love Tides," Andie said.

"Good. We don't want to end up like Sadie Thompson."

"What happened to Sadie Thompson?" Andie looked concerned.

"Nothing yet. But I heard that the family is having trouble coming up with the fee."

"Huh. The daughter does seem a bit... unreasonable."

"Really? You know her?"

"No. I peeked into Sadie's room, you know, because Mom keeps talking about her, and she started up a conversation. Her daughter came by and practically kicked me out."

"Really? Maybe she's under a lot of stress about paying the fees. If you ask me, she should sell that old place. Sadie lived there by herself for decades, and now it's empty and falling apart." Jane looked around the foyer. Tides wasn't in the best condition either. She'd considered selling for a brief second, but Tides had been in her family for generations, and besides, she'd promised her mother she would never sell. Maybe Sadie's daughter felt the same.

"Yeah, I suppose. We're lucky that things are picking up for us. The weddings were a great idea, and everyone seems to love Cooper." Andie bent down to pet the dog, who had been lying near the door.

"Who wouldn't?"

"Plus having Cooper means that Mike comes around often." Andie looked at Jane out of the corner of her eye, and Jane's cheeks heated.

"I hope he doesn't want Cooper back when he gets a place here."

"I'm sure he won't do anything that you wouldn't like."

"I wouldn't be too sure about that."

Andie frowned. "What do you mean?"

"Oh, nothing. It's just that we really don't know each other, and everything is so new. I don't want to make any assumptions," Jane said. Somehow voicing her concerns made her feel a lot better.

"I understand. I don't think you have anything to worry about. Speaking of which, what's going on with Maxi? I gave her some advice earlier, and I hope I didn't do the wrong thing."

"You did?"

"Yeah." Andie grimaced. "She confided in me that she thought her husband was cheating and she was going to move into the cottage, and I told her it was the right thing to do. I hope that I said the right thing."

"Well, I think you did, given the circumstances, but it turns out James wasn't cheating." Jane told Andie about the misunderstanding and how they were helping James so he could get Maxi back.

"Oh gosh, if I had known, I wouldn't have encouraged her," Andie said.

Jane laid her hand on Andie's arm. "It's okay. We thought he was cheating too."

"Oh good. I'm glad he wasn't cheating. Is she going back to him?"

"Let's hope. Right now I think she's tasting her freedom and doesn't want to go back to their old relationship."

"That makes sense." Andie looked thoughtful. Jane wanted to ask if something was on her mind, but her sense that Andie wasn't ready to tell her was proven correct when Andie plucked the car keys off the desk. "Okay then, if you don't need me here, I have something I need to do before I visit Mom at Tall Pines."

Andie took a detour on the way to Tall Pines. As she drove, she thought about what Jane had said about Maxi finding her way and not wanting to go back to her old life. Andie was experiencing something similar.

She was excited for the visit, not just to see her mother but also because Mae was bringing her figurines in for Andie to evaluate. For some reason, the idea of helping these folks was very appealing.

But the mention of Sadie Thompson's house had piqued her interest. She remembered the house that sat high up on a cliff from when she was a kid. Back then it hadn't been run-down, or if it had, she hadn't noticed. She'd been into other things, like Shane Flannery. But the history of the house was appealing, and she wanted to know more. She wanted to go inside and see the old family treasures. Maybe she could help Sadie Thompson like she was helping Mae and Gloria?

She tried to replace the thoughts of Shane that were stuck in her head with thoughts of the old house, but Shane stuck around. Remembering him as they were back in the day. He'd been cute back then, but he'd gotten even more appealing as he'd aged. Not for the first time, Andie wondered if she'd made a mistake back then in dumping him after his proposal and running off to college. It hadn't been because she didn't love him. It had been because she was afraid. Afraid that he'd never come back from the Navy. Afraid that she'd never make anything of herself if she stayed in Lobster Bay.

Oh well, it was water under the bridge now. Shane hadn't expressed an interest in her. He didn't seem mad. He actually didn't even give any indication that he remembered how close they'd been. That was decades ago, and he'd been married and had kids and even a grandkid now. How could she expect him to remember their teen relationship?

Rounding a corner, the Thompson house came into view. Sitting on a cliff, it looked out at the ocean like a widow awaiting a sea captain's return. It was much as Andie remembered, except it did need a good paint job. A shutter hung askew on one of the upper-floor windows, and Andie imagined it banging against the house in a strong wind. The windows were dark, the grounds overgrown. The house screamed of empty silence.

What would happen to it? Surely Sadie's daughter, Emily, wouldn't just let it rot there? She must not have the money to fix it up. Maybe she was waiting for Sadie to die and she could use insurance money. Andie would love to ask, but judging by the way Emily had acted when she'd found Andie in her mother's room, the woman wasn't going to be easy to make friends with.

Andie turned around and headed back to town, thoughts of Maxi crossing her mind. *Had* she done the right thing to encourage her? Probably not, since James didn't cheat, but maybe all the things Jane and Claire were doing to bring James on board with Maxi's dreams would be a new beginning for them. Maxi leaving could be a blessing in disguise. Andie hoped so. She liked Maxi and wanted to see her happy.

She was starting to get attached to people and to the

town. When Jane had come into the foyer and seen her on the phone with Courtney, the bridezilla, Andie had worried Jane might be mad that Andie had taken it upon herself to talk to the bride. But Jane had been relieved. Andie had felt proud to help smooth things over with Courtney and her mother, Marilyn, who had dominated the conversation. Andie actually had a feeling that Courtney might have been more easygoing if not for her mother butting in, but what could you do? Good thing Andie had helped out, though. Jane was right—she didn't have the personality for it. She got flustered too easily.

Andie liked being a part of the team at Tides, but that would never be enough for her. She needed something else to do.

Almost as if it had a mind of its own, her rental car turned toward Main Street. She drove past the shops with their cheery awnings and flower-laden window boxes, passing a cute boutique shop, a florist, a hairdresser, and then the antiques shop. Its door was closed, its window boxes empty, and the lights off.

The building was a decent size and in a good section of town. Andie found herself wondering what the apartment above looked like. Was it outdated? In need of major work? Her room at Tides was getting a bit small, and it was also a room they could rent out. With the current upswing in guests, it didn't make sense for her to take up that space.

If she decided to stay in Lobster Bay, buying the antiques shop and apartment would be a perfect solution for her. Excitement rippled through her as she weighed thoughts of staying with thoughts of going back. Suddenly and with much clarity, she had a clear winner. She knew exactly what she wanted to do.

CHAPTER FIFTEEN

The Purple Blueberry was everything Maxi imagined it would be. Awash in vibrant tones, the outdoor bar was dotted with round tables shaded with colorful umbrellas. Strings of lights with large filament exposed bulbs were strung around the tall purple fence that blocked the bar from the neighboring business. Artwork hung on the fence and the walls of the building. Inside was another bar and more tables, but it was a gorgeous evening and the crowd was outside.

Maxi sat at a small table, taking it all in as she sampled a glass of pinot noir from a local winery. The buzz of conversation, the excitement of creative energy, the colorful casual outfits. This was what her life had been missing.

"Maxi, great to see you here!" Chandler Vanbeck rushed over, making Maxi feel a little uncomfortable.

She didn't want him to think she'd come looking for him. "Mind if I join you?"

"Of course not." Maxi gestured toward the empty chair across from her.

"So how are the paintings coming along?" Chandler relaxed back in his chair, crossing his ankle over one knee and taking a sip of his white wine. He was wearing cargo shorts and a T-shirt with a colorful artsy dog face on it. Quite a different look from their previous meeting, where he'd worn business-casual chinos and a button-down shirt.

"Good. Great actually. I'm almost done with the second one, so it should be no problem to have three ready for the opening." She couldn't believe that she was casually talking about having her artwork at a gallery opening.

"Perfect! I think you'll be surprised at the attention your work gets." Chandler leaned forward, a little too close, causing Maxi to lean back to maintain the distance.

Was he flirting? She wasn't sure if she liked being flirted with, especially now that she'd been so wrong about James. She'd been second-guessing her decision to stay at the cottage and feeling bad about the way she'd suspected her husband. Then again, James hadn't exactly acted like he would welcome her back with open arms. Maybe he was mad at the way she'd acted. She wouldn't blame him if he was.

"I'm looking forward to it. I'm surprised I got back into painting so easily. It's been years."

"You're a natural. I could tell by that sketch I saw. Can't wait to see the paintings."

A woman who Maxi recognized as the one she was introduced to at the diner drifted up to their table. Today she was wearing a bright-yellow linen shirt and white pedal pushers. She had gigantic daisy earrings and necklace to match. Overly large white-rimmed sunglasses completed the outfit. "Hello there. Maxi, right?"

Maxi nodded. "And you're Muriel?"

"Yes! How lovely of you to remember." She glanced at an empty seat. "May I?"

"Please do." Maxi felt a lot better now that it wasn't just her and Chandler. It wasn't that he was entirely unpleasant. Actually, he was rather handsome. And he'd been so nice to her. She might have welcomed his flirtation if things were different, but when she thought about having a man in her life, all she could think of was James.

"Chandler tells me you're a new artist." Muriel gave Maxi a smile of encouragement. "You must be good if he's including you in the opening."

Maxi blushed. "I'm sort of new. I used to paint a lot when I was younger, but then I got married, had a family..."

"Oh, I know what you mean. That's one benefit of

getting older. You finally have time to do what *you* want."

Maxi nodded her agreement. She liked Muriel. The woman was outgoing, smart, pleasant.

A familiar figure hovering around the edge of the tables caught her eye.

James? Except he wasn't wearing his usual clothes. He was dressed down, casual. Handsome. Their eyes met, and Maxi's heart flipped. For a second, she was transported back to their younger days when they were both more carefree. James looked good, better than he had in years.

Maxi waved him over, and Muriel turned. "Who is that?"

"My husband." Maxi couldn't help her voice rising an octave at the end as if it were a question.

"Hi." James stood beside her at the table, looking nervous.

"What are you doing here?" Maxi asked.

"Oh, just wanted to check it out." James frowned at Chandler. Maxi wondered if he was jealous.

"James, this is Chandler Vanbeck—he owns the new art gallery—and this is Muriel Fox."

"I hear your wife is quite an artist," Muriel said to James.

"Yes. So do I." James's odd reply caused Muriel to frown. "I mean, she hasn't had a chance to do it for a while. When we were younger, she was quite good."

"Would you like to sit?" Maxi asked. "We could pull over a chair from that table."

"No... I... um... I have to be somewhere else," James stammered. "I was passing by and saw you so figured I'd say hi."

"Okay." Why was James acting so strange? Probably because he hadn't expected her to be at the Purple Blueberry. But why was *he* here? Was he really just passing by? Her earlier suspicions of him and Sandee bubbled up, but that couldn't be true. Jane and Claire had assured her that was a misunderstanding.

James pecked her cheek and squeezed her arm, and before she could think any more about it, he walked away.

Muriel turned in her chair and slid the sunglasses down her nose as she watched him walk away. "Your husband is quite handsome. Both coming and going."

"I know." Maxi was also watching James leave.

Chandler cleared his throat, and both women switched their gaze from James's retreating behind to Chandler.

"Don't worry, dear, you're handsome too," Muriel assured him.

"Thank you." He held up his empty wine glass. "And with that, I think I'll go get a refill. Would you ladies like one?"

They shook their heads. Both of them had half-full glasses.

Chandler left, and Muriel put her sunglasses on the table then looked at Maxi. "Kind of odd that your husband didn't sit with us."

Was it that obvious, or was Muriel just really perceptive? Maxi sighed. "We're kind of going through a rough patch."

Muriel patted her arm. "I think I know what you mean. You're branching out, doing things for yourself for once. You said you hadn't painted in decades because you set it aside to raise your family. Now you're having *you* time, and it's adding a different dynamic."

"It's not just that." Maxi glanced at Chandler. She felt awkward talking about her personal problems to a stranger, but Muriel had a way of making one feel as if they'd been friends for ages. Maxi had a feeling that Muriel would understand exactly where she was coming from. "We were having trouble before. Our relationship was distant. That's what prompted me to go my own way." She didn't want to tell her how she'd wrongfully suspected the cheating. It was embarrassing. "We've grown apart since the kids left."

Muriel's left brow quirked up. "Well, if you ask me, that's not a man that wants to stay apart."

"Really?" Maxi glanced in the direction James had taken, but he was gone. "Maybe it's for the best. I'm afraid if we go back to our old ways, I'll lose this new part of me. If I have to choose, I'm not sure if I would choose my old life or my new."

Muriel gave her a funny look. "Who says you have to choose?"

Maxi frowned. "I don't know. James never really encouraged me to do creative things before. Somehow, I feel like I have this one opportunity to live out my dreams, and I don't want to waste it."

Muriel shrugged and took a sip of wine. "I can certainly understand that, but maybe you can find a way to blend the old with the new and have it all."

James's mind whirred as he wandered through the crowd of tourists with their colorful summer shirts, flip-flops, and half-eaten ice cream cones. He didn't know what he'd expected, but things hadn't gone quite as James had planned at the Purple Blueberry.

Who was that guy—Chandler—sitting with Maxi? Okay, maybe he was reading too much into that. They had only been sitting at a table together, and it wasn't just the two of them. Another woman had been there. For all James knew, the man and woman were a couple. Maybe they were all just friends. But the vibe the man was giving off wasn't that of a friend. And the way he looked at Maxi told James the man's intentions were more than just friendly.

He'd messed up. The whole plan was to join Maxi, loosen up, have a good time, and reconnect. But the presence of this Chandler guy had thrown him for a loop, and James had never been good at thinking on his feet. In fact, this whole misunderstanding had started because he couldn't respond to Maxi's question about how he'd ignored her downtown when he'd been trying to keep Picasso as a surprise.

What he should have done was sat right down at the table and joined in. Pretended to be at ease in Maxi's artsy world. Had that really become her world so quickly? Would he ever fit in? Sally would probably say he never would if he didn't try. And now he'd screwed up trying.

Maxi had invited him to join them, which probably meant that Chandler was just a friend. If James could only have thought that through faster, he would have sat down. Right now he could be drinking wine with Maxi. Instead he was walking down the street alone, and she was sitting back at the Purple Blueberry with Chandler. It was too late to go back now. He'd already said he was just passing by. Too late to fix what he should have done.

Should have, would have, could have. Hopefully he hadn't blown his chances.

CHAPTER SIXTEEN

The next morning, James got a call from Jane.

"How did it go at the Purple Blueberry?" Jane's tone was one of curious optimism.

"She was with a guy." James walked through the bedroom, looking on the bed for Picasso. The cat hadn't eaten his breakfast, and James hadn't seen him this morning. He was starting to get worried.

"A guy? What do you mean? I know for a fact Maxi doesn't have a boyfriend," Jane said.

James felt a pang of guilt at suspecting she did. "I know, but it threw me. She was at a table with this guy, Chandler, and a woman named Muriel."

Jane sighed. "Chandler is the art gallery guy. They were probably talking business."

"She did invite me to stay, but I got all flustered

about the guy. I didn't stay." James opened the closet and looked inside. No cat. "Guess I messed up."

"No. You just missed an opportunity to spend time with her and reconnect. Don't worry. There will be others. In fact, I have a great idea on how you and Maxi can spend a lot of time together."

"You do?"

"Yes. We have a table for friends at the wedding on Saturday, and you're invited."

"I am? I don't even know the bride and groom." James peeked into his office. Picasso had taken to pushing his books off the bookshelf and lying in the empty space, but the cat wasn't there.

"You don't need to. All you need is Maxi and a romantic setting."

James felt nervous. What if Maxi didn't want him there? What if he messed up again? "I don't know. What if she brings that guy?"

"Don't worry. She won't. She's not interested in him. She loves you and wants you back, but she also wants to still be able to continue with her creative endeavors. You want her to do that, don't you?"

"Yes, of course." James was kicking himself for not nurturing Maxi's creative side sooner. Whatever she wanted, he was good with it as long as she was happy.

"And you're going to the gallery opening, right? Her work will be in there."

"Should I?" James peeked into the bathroom, pulling the shower curtain aside. No Picasso.

Jane sighed. Probably at his cluelessness. Maxi had been the only woman he'd seriously dated, and apparently, in addition to lessons on how to dress, he needed lessons on how to win a woman over. Maybe he should consult with Sally.

"Yes, you should go. It will be a perfect way to show Maxi that you support her new life," Jane said.

"Okay, I'll be there."

"Great, see you then. And don't worry. Maxi will come around, and you guys will be back together and stronger than ever."

Jane hung up, and James stared at the phone. He hoped she was right.

A gagging sound had him racing to the bedroom. It was coming from the bed. The cat wasn't on top of the bed, but...

"Picasso?" James peered under the bed skirt, and his heart sank.

Picasso was crouched down like a rabbit, his eyes mere slits. He reminded James of the way the kids looked when they had the flu.

"Are you okay, little buddy?" James lay on the floor and reached in for the cat. Picasso did not resist, a sure sign that something was dreadfully wrong.

James pulled him into his lap and leaned his back against the bed, trying to comfort the cat, but Picasso wanted none of it. He tried to slink away but only made it a few feet before he started the most ungodly heaving and choking noises James had ever heard.

Oh no! What was happening? Should he call the vet?

Picasso stopped choking and glared at James. James's heart twisted. He'd become incredibly attached to the cat in the few days he'd been here. If something happened to him, he didn't know what he would do. He needed to call the vet, but in the meantime, he racked his brain for something he could do to ease the poor thing's suffering.

The cashmere sweater vest!

James leapt up, grabbed the vest out of the drawer, then made a little nest on the floor for Picasso, who was starting with the heaving again. The cat eyed the vest, hobbled over to the middle, his stomach lurching, and then...

Gak!

Picasso's mouth opened wide, and out came an impossibly large tube of compacted hair. A hairball?

It landed on the white trim of James's sweater vest, staining it cat-food yellow.

Picasso shook his head then sat on his haunches and proceeded to groom himself. He'd apparently recovered from the ordeal quickly. James's sweater, on the other hand, had not.

James got a paper towel and disposed of the

disgusting hairball. When he came back, Picasso was fast asleep, curled up in the middle of the sweater-vest nest. James couldn't help but smile. The sweater might be ruined, but Picasso was okay.

Jane hung up and looked around the foyer at Tides. She'd done her good deed for the day in calling James. Cooper thought so, too, judging by the way he was looking up at her approvingly.

"Don't worry, boy. They'll find their way back to each other."

Woof!

Jane took a deep breath and looked around the lobby. She needed to focus on getting this place in perfect order for the wedding. Her mother had always said that making a good first impression was important.

"Maybe I should put out some coffee and pastries for when people check in. Brenda will be happy to make something special, and I can hit up Claire for some treats from Sandcastles."

Cooper trotted over to the narrow mahogany side-board against the stairway wall. Jane had always loved that piece with its richly carved grapes and white marble top. "You're right, that's a perfect spot."

She cleared her grandmother's flow blue china plates, which stood in little easels, off the top of the sideboard and put them carefully in the glass-front china cabinet in the dining room. Cooper trotted around behind her, watching patiently, then followed her back out into the lobby.

"Now what? Flowers? Maybe if we place some of Nona's vases around with flowers from the garden..." Jane went to the window beside the door and looked out at the garden. Andie had done an amazing job with it in the few weeks she'd been here, and it was thick with colorful flowers. The hummingbird feeders Andie had pulled out of storage sat filled with red liquid, and iridescent green birds zoomed around them.

Andie herself was at the arbor, probably trying to figure out how to get the pink roses the bride had requested. "Let's go out and talk to Andie about the flower vases, and we can get an update on the arbor while we're at it."

Cooper didn't have to be told twice about an opportunity to go outside. He was already at the door before Jane even finished the sentence.

Andie trimmed a few dead leaves from the rosebush at the base of the arbor and eyed the hanging baskets loaded with miniature roses. If she could place those in strategic spots then weave in some fresh-cut roses the day of the wedding, the arbor would look fantastic. She just needed someone to make some adjustments to the arbor so she could hang and weave.

Woof!

Cooper bounded over, and Andie knelt to pet him.

"Those are pretty." Jane gestured to the hanging baskets. "I bet this will look great when you're done."

Andie stood. "Let's hope. I need some adjustments to the arbor, though. Did you talk to anyone about doing that?"

"Sally is going to take care of that today," Jane said.

"Oh great." Hadn't Jane said that Shane was going to do that? Andie wasn't exactly disappointed—Sally would do a good job—but she had to admit she was kind of hoping for Shane. Oh well, she had more important things to think about right now. "How are the centerpieces coming along?"

"Great! Maxi finished painting the candles for us and is bringing them over tomorrow morning. She's focusing on finishing her painting for the gallery opening today." Jane fingered a delicate petal of one of the roses that climbed up the arbor. "You are going to the opening, right?"

"Of course, I wouldn't miss it."

"You can come with Mike and me if you want."

"Thanks, I'd like that." It felt good to be included, and it was nice of Jane to think of her. "How are things going with Maxi and James?"

Jane sighed. "Not easy. He seems to be worried that Chandler has designs on Maxi."

"Chandler? I doubt that. He usually goes for ditzy blondes." Andie thought for a minute. "But he did seem really interested in Maxi. I figured it was just because of the sketch he saw, but maybe not? She is attractive. You don't think she's interested in him, do you?"

"No, definitely not. She loves James." Jane's phone pinged, and she pulled it out of her pocket, her face lighting up. "It's Mike. He wants me to go look at condos with him. Says he needs a second opinion."

"Sounds serious." Andie wiggled her brows.

Jane blushed. "I'm not moving in with him, if that's what you mean."

"Why not? You guys make a great couple."

Jane's smile faded, and she gazed out at the ocean. "Well, you never know. I guess for now it doesn't hurt to approve of his condo. Besides, it's fun to look at places. Can we get together when I get back to go over more plans for the wedding?"

"Of course. I'll be here." Andie watched her sister walk away. Things were getting a bit complicated in Lobster Bay. Maxi and James's relationship could have a wrinkle if Chandler was in the mix, and why did Jane suddenly seem concerned about her relationship with Mike? Andie shook her head and went back to her work. Hopefully everything would work out fine for everyone.

$\mathcal{M}$ike liked the condo at Boulder Hills. It was an end unit with two bedrooms and a large deck in the back. The yard was private, too, fenced off from the abutting unit with a tall fence. It didn't have a water view, but those condos were out of his price range.

"I thought you might like the kitchen island and the window over the sink looking out at the woods." Mike pointed the features out to Jane. Sure, he liked them, too, but he really wanted to be sure it was a place where she could see herself spending a lot of time.

"Those are good features. But do *you* like them?"

"Yep. Very nice." Mike also liked the simple clean lines of the place. They sort of reminded him of Jane. The condo suited her personality—not pretentious or frilly.

"Are you going to take up cooking?" Jane teased. It was well-known that Mike could barely pour cereal. That was why he'd bartered with Jane for breakfast at Tides every morning in return for creating the website for the inn. Well, *one* of the reasons. The other was to see Jane, of course.

"I was thinking maybe you'd come over and cook."

Jane frowned. "Maybe you should see if the kitchen suits Brenda. She's better at it than I am."

"Well, I hope she likes it, because I think I like this one the best," Mike said. They'd looked at three condos already, and he did like this one but wanted to pick the one Jane liked.

Jane turned to the realtor. "Do they allow dogs?"

"Yes, one dog per unit. I saw the golden in your car. Is it yours?" she asked Mike.

"No, he's Jane's, but he will be visiting a lot." Mike glanced at Jane. "Hopefully."

Mike didn't regret his decision to let Jane adopt Cooper. Cooper and Jane had bonded, and she brought Cooper to see Gramps often. Plus, if things worked out the way Mike wanted, he'd be seeing Cooper almost as much as if he did live here. And maybe eventually...

His phone vibrated, and he pulled it out of his pocket and turned it off without looking. Truth be told, he was afraid to look. Tiffany had texted him a few times about meeting up, since she was in town for the art gallery opening. Hopefully she would get the message that he didn't want to get together at all.

Jane glanced at his phone, a frown creasing her brow. "We're still going to the gallery opening tomorrow night, right?"

How odd she would mention that when it was the very thing Mike was worrying about. How would Tiffany react when she saw Mike with Jane? Would she cause a scene? Maybe Mike was making too much of this. Tiffany was probably over him and just wanted to say hi.

"Of course. I wouldn't miss it."

"Good. I invited Andie to go with us. You don't mind, do you?"

"Not at all. Whatever you want is good for me."

"Great." Jane took another turn around the condo. "You know, I think this one is my favorite too."

Maxi cradled Rembrandt in her arms and stood back to admire her painting. It was the last one for the art gallery opening, and it was almost finished.

Stepping away, she glanced toward the ocean and took a deep breath of sea air to quell her nerves. Even though she had done her best work, she was still nervous about the gallery opening. Would people like her work? How would it stack up against the other artists on display?

"What do you think, Rembrandt?" She put the cat down and watched as he walked the perimeter of the patio. He was crouched low, moving slowly. She didn't let him outside very much and only under strict supervision, so his little kitten eyes were wide with delight. Maybe if she and James got their own place, she would make some kind of fence or enclosure so Rembrandt could go outside and still be safe.

She and James? What would their life be like going forward? Did they even have a future, or had Maxi ruined it?

She'd been shocked to see him at the Purple Blueberry, but why didn't he stay? She didn't buy his story that he was on his way somewhere else and saw her so stopped in.

He'd looked good in more casual attire. Maxi suspected that Jane and Claire had had something to do with that. Had they been coaching him? She wouldn't have a chance to ask them today. She had to finish the painting and wasn't allowing herself to do anything else until she did.

The thought of James going to all that effort for her warmed her heart. Should she call him? No, that would be a distraction from her task of painting. And besides, she was a little nervous now because he'd left so abruptly. Maybe he'd decided that hanging out with the artsy crowd and frequenting places like the Purple Blue-berry really wasn't his thing. If that were the case, did that mean they couldn't be together? Maxi didn't want to give up her new life, but she also didn't want to give up James.

Mew!

Rembrandt was sitting at the slider, looking inside. He probably wanted to graze at his food bowl. She'd never seen a cat eat so much!

She opened the slider, and he scooted inside. Then she turned to the painting and picked up the brush. She'd told Chandler she would drop the paintings off this afternoon. She'd better get those final touches in soon so it would have time to dry.

Jane watched as Andie pushed the centerpiece a smidge to the left. They were out on the back deck of Tides, setting up the table-scape for the reception so they could have something to show Courtney and her mother. They weren't arriving for another day, but Jane didn't want to leave it to the last minute.

Jane and Andie had been moving things around, standing back. Moving more things. Cooper was apparently uninterested, lying on the edge of the deck near the railing, the ocean breeze ruffling his golden fur.

Andie stepped back and tilted her head as she assessed the arrangement. "There, I think that's perfect."

The table did look perfect with the backdrop of the ocean, the crisp white cloth, sparkling cut crystal wine glasses, white porcelain gold-rimmed dinner plates, and the white flower centerpiece with blue ribbon.

"I agree," Jane said, glad that all the moving about was done. She honestly didn't see how moving the knife one millimeter to the left made a big difference, but Andie knew more about this stuff than she did, so she'd deferred to her sister's expertise.

"We just need the candles," Andie said.

"Maxi is bringing those tomorrow morning." Jane glanced over toward the area where the tent would be set up on the morning of the wedding. Since the wedding was an evening affair, the tent rental place had advised they do the setup that morning instead of the day before.

Andie put her arm around Jane's shoulders and gave her a squeeze. "Don't worry. Everything will be fine."

"I suppose. It's just that Courtney is so picky." Jane's gaze drifted to the bathhouse, with its quaint sailboat shutters and colorful window boxes. Andie had loaded them with flowers, and they'd spruce up the inside of the bathhouse with giant conch shells, starfish, and sea glass on the towel shelves and vanities. Her gaze drifted to the arbor. "Did you figure out a method for the roses?"

"Sally had a hard time figuring what to do, but in the end, we figured it out. She said Shane would have been better at it, but he was busy."

Jane flicked her gaze to her sister, to something unreadable reflected in her hazel eyes. "Disappointed?"

Andie blushed and looked away. "No, of course not. Sally did a great job. It's going to look fantastic."

"I'm sure it is." Jane decided to press her luck. Andie was opening up lately, and she felt like she could get more personal. "So what happened with you and Shane back then? I was too young and self-involved to pay attention. He seems like a really nice guy. And not too hard on the eyes either."

Andie laughed. "He did age well. I guess our lives just weren't heading in the same direction. He was going into the navy, and I wanted to be in the city." She avoided eye contact, looking out at the ocean.

"Seems like maybe now your lives are different. Maybe you're going in the same direction," Jane said softly.

Andie pursed her lips as if she was ready to protest, but then her face softened. Her expression turned teasing. "So, tell me how the condo shopping went with Mike."

Now it was Jane's turn to blush. "I liked the last one we looked at today. It was just on the edge of town in Boulder Hills. The development is pretty, lots of nice landscaping."

"Is that where the old Swenson farm used to be?"

Jane nodded. While she hated the idea that an old farm was no longer in existence, they had made a nice neighborhood out of it.

"Did Mike like it?"

"I think so. He seemed more interested in finding out if I liked it."

Andie smirked. "Of course he did."

Jane frowned. "Why?"

Andie shook her head. "Sis, I think I need to take you under my wing in the relationship department. You're kind of naive. Mike wants you to like it because he's hoping you'll spend a lot of time there."

"Oh, really?" Jane's heart fluttered, and she felt flustered. She'd been hoping that was the reason but was also nervous if it was.

"Yeah, any fool can see that." Andie squeezed her hand. "I'm happy for you. Don't worry. Just enjoy it. He's a good guy."

"Yeah, he is, except..."

Andie's expression turned concerned. "What?"

"I don't know. The other day at Tall Pines, he got this weird phone call from back home, and he seemed concerned after. He said it was nothing, but I got the impression he was hiding something."

"Are you sure?" Andie asked. "He doesn't seem like the type. Maybe you're just being paranoid."

Jane turned back to the table and moved a fork a centimeter to the right. "Maybe. You're probably right."

Setting her focus back on the table, she pushed thoughts of Mike aside. She had a lot more pressing matters to worry about.

CHAPTER EIGHTEEN

*A*ndie's life was becoming more and more about Lobster Bay and less and less about New York City. She now found the ocean breeze much more appealing than the city smog, and working in the garden at Tides and dealing with the guests had given her back her sense of family pride. Not to mention that visits with her mother had become even more precious now that Addie's memory was failing.

She'd been surprised to discover that helping the residents at Tall Pines with their antiques so that they didn't get ripped off by the unscrupulous Damien Carruthers was more rewarding than any big find she might have scored in the antique world.

When she'd visited her mother at Tall Pines the day before, Andie had sought out Rita to ask if she could look at the antique shop and apartment. She'd awakened to find a message from a realtor. She could view the shop and apartment this morning if she wanted.

She showered and rushed downstairs to grab some breakfast before heading to the appointment. Brenda was in her glory, anticipating an inn full of guests to cook for.

"Try this New Mexican egg scramble." Brenda dished up a colorful plate of eggs with peppers, onions, and beans and handed it to Andie.

They were fluffy, spicy, and delicious. "Fabulous. Maybe some sour cream on the side?" Andie said as she shoveled the rest in and picked up her car keys. She only had a few minutes to spare.

Andie ran into Maxi in the foyer. She was just coming in the front door, her arms full of two dozen candles painted with blue stripes.

"Those look great." Andie took one and examined it. She had a good eye for color, and it looked like a perfect match for the bridesmaid colors.

"Thanks. I hope they pass muster. I hear the bridezilla is coming tomorrow."

"Yeah. Jane's on pins and needles, but I think she'll love everything. It's all coming together." Andie hoped. "How are you doing? Are you ready for the art gallery opening?"

Maxi beamed. "It's all very exciting and overwhelming. But I finished the paintings, so I'm as ready as I'll ever be. Are you going?"

"Of course, I wouldn't miss it." Andie cocked her head. "And how are other things going?" Andie was in a hurry to see the antiques store, but she genuinely cared about Maxi. The realtor would wait a few minutes, especially if they wanted their commission.

Maxi sighed. "You mean with James? I don't know what to do there. It seems like he's trying to win me back."

"That doesn't seem like a bad thing."

"No, but I think Claire and Jane have something to do with that. Though now that I know the truth, I guess I might have overreacted. I owe him, since I acted like a jerk. But I'm still reluctant to give up my new life." Maxi shrugged. "Honestly, I've been so focused on finishing the paintings, I haven't thought much about it. Now I need to straighten out the rest of my life."

"Do you still love him?" Andie asked.

Maxi nodded. "I do. It's just that things are different now. I think we need to approach our relationship carefully so that we mend it in the right way. But I can't imagine being with anyone else. Especially since Chandler seems a little flirty."

"Chandler was hitting on you?"

Maxi frowned. "I don't know if I'd say that. I'm so out of touch with dating, I don't know if I'd recognize it if someone were hitting on me. But it seems like he's interested, and it's making it a bit awkward with the gallery and all. But it's probably my imagination. Why would anyone be interested in me?"

"I didn't mean it that way. Any guy would be lucky to have you," Andie said sincerely. "Chandler usually goes for younger blondes with, um... not as many brains. You're smart and sophisticated."

Maxi blushed. "Thanks. I guess maybe I'm getting a little full of myself."

"Not at all. A woman knows when a guy is flirting. But you shouldn't let that impact any of your decisions with the art gallery, or your career. Just send Chandler the signal you aren't interested. I'm sure he wouldn't take away any opportunities because of that." Andie hoped he wouldn't. She'd known Chandler a long time and had never heard of him being a jerk in that way.

"I'm not even sure I know how to send those signals. I guess I'll be asking for a lot of advice at coffee this morning." Maxi's gaze drifted to the keys Andie was jangling in her hand. "Are you heading out somewhere?"

"Yeah. I have a meeting." Andie didn't want to tell anyone about the antique store yet. She hadn't even mentioned it to Jane, and she wasn't one hundred percent sure she would rent it. No sense in talking about it until she'd made the final decision, and when she did, Jane should be the first to know. "I do have to run. We'll catch up later? And good luck tonight if I don't see you before the opening. Break a leg!"

Andie rushed out to her rental. That was another thing. If she decided to stay, she'd have to buy a car. She didn't have one in New York. Better to make the decision sooner—the rental cost a lot. She was glad Maxi was going to work things out with James and glad Jane, Maxi, and Claire had one another to bounce things off of. She didn't want to horn in on their coffee hour, but it would be nice to be invited ... if only just once.

CHAPTER NINETEEN

The antique store was crammed full. Depression glass, mahogany furniture, oriental rugs. Andie ran her finger along a half inch of dust that had accumulated on an oak roll-top desk that looked to be from the late 1800s.

"So, as you see, it's fully stocked already!" the perky realtor, Autumn Blaisedale, said in a chipper voice that grated on Andie. She hadn't had much choice in who she chose as an agent, though. There were only a few realtors in Lobster Bay, and Andie had made sure not to use the infamous husband-stealing Sandee Harris. Even if the woman hadn't been cheating with James, she *had* cheated with Claire's husband. "This inventory must be worth tens of thousands."

Irritating voice or not, she had a point. Though Andie wasn't scrutinizing every item, her experienced eye did pick out a few very nice pieces. Most were fairly common, but that sort of thing appealed to many shoppers. Not everyone was in the market for a rare Ming dynasty vase. As she looked at the items, her pulse quickened. Excitement rippled through her as she pictured herself sorting through the inventory, handling the items, going on house calls in some of the old houses in Lobster Bay, and attending antique auctions.

But she didn't want to get too excited, lest the chirpy realtor smell an opportunity to jack up the selling price and thus her commission. "It seems adequate."

Chirpy's smile dimmed a few watts. "Would you like to see the apartment?"

Andie followed her upstairs. She'd expected a space that was old-fashioned with braided rugs and hand-crocheted doilies, but the upstairs area was a pleasant surprise. It had high ceilings, exposed brick walls, and tall windows that let in tons of natural light. The living area was open to the kitchen and boasted black granite counters with gray cabinets. The original wide pine floors were in good condition. Rita had good taste.

The place boasted two bedrooms, the one in the back with a distant view of the ocean over the rooftops of the smaller buildings behind it. The bathrooms could have used a bit of an upgrade but were serviceable.

Andie could see herself living there. It already felt like home.

"And the hair salon next door is very convenient.

They give the best pedicures and amazing cuts." Chirpy fluffed her short bob. "Such a cute family business, three generations."

Andie looked out the window to see a woman with long curly gray hair sweeping up in front of the shop. It did look appealing with its gigantic scissors sign and large plants in front. She pulled her own long ponytail over her shoulder, wondering if it might be time for a shorter cut. Jane's hair looked so cute in its short pixie style, but Andie had had long hair her whole life. She wouldn't feel like herself if she cut it. The gray hairs coming in, on the other hand, might need a touch-up.

"So what do you think?" Autumn pulled some papers out of her leather briefcase. "Rita is anxious to sell and gave me the financials for the shop. It's been out of business for five years now, but the numbers should still be fairly relevant."

Andie would do her due diligence on the shop later to make sure it was in the black. She didn't need to make a ton of money and still wanted to help Jane at Tides part-time.

"Thanks." Andie took the papers and did a slow turn around the room. "So, what do you think Rita's best price is?"

❧

Maxi sat at one of the outdoor café tables at Sandcastles

with a blueberry muffin so fresh the steam came out of it when she cut it open. Next to the muffin was a dark roast coffee, but the best part was that she was with her two best friends, Claire and Jane.

Could life get any better? Only if she sold a painting at the gallery opening.

"I'm so excited for the gallery opening tonight!" Claire slathered butter on her muffin, and it immediately started to melt.

"Me, too," Maxi said. "Okay, mostly I'm nervous."

"You'll be fine," Jane assured. "And the candles came out perfect."

"The table-scape looked amazing, and Claire's cake is perfect. I'm sure your bride is going to love it," Maxi said. Not everything was about her. Jane had something important going on in her life too. Also, when Maxi had dropped off the candlesticks earlier that morning, she'd seen a sample of Claire's frosted sandcastle cake. The color had almost been an exact match.

Claire let out a breath. "I hope so. I tried to match the frosting color as much as I could."

"It's almost identical," Maxi said. "I'm pretty good with color."

"Andie said so too." Jane reached for the other half of her muffin.

"So what's going on with Andie? She's been around for a while now. Is she staying in town?" Maxi had been about to ask her to join them for coffee when she'd bumped into her in the lobby at Tides but then Andie rushed off.

Jane shrugged. "She hasn't said. But it's been really nice having her. I feel like we've reconnected."

"I was thinking it might be nice to ask her to join our morning coffee meetings," Maxi said. "I was going to ask this morning, but she was rushing off somewhere. Do you guys mind?"

"Not at all." Claire turned to Jane. "You don't mind, do you?"

"No. I should have thought of it earlier, but I kept expecting her to leave town abruptly."

"She seems to be settling in." Maxi sipped her coffee, looking at her friends over the rim of the mug. They were watching her expectantly. "Okay, I know you guys are dying to ask about James. The truth is I've been busy with the paintings, and maybe I've been using that as an excuse not to think about our relationship too. I'm actually not sure what to do."

"Have you talked to him?"

"Not since I saw him at the Purple Blueberry." Maxi put the coffee mug down and leaned forward to pet Cooper, who had been lying at Jane's feet. "By the way, don't think I don't know that you both put him up to that... and have you been dressing him too? I noticed he had an outfit that was less..."

"Stodgy?" Claire supplied, and the three of them burst out laughing.

"I guess you might say that." Maxi admitted that James had taken to going a bit overboard with the business attire.

"I hope you don't think we were going behind your back." Jane's face softened. "He really is in a bad way."

"Once we were convinced he didn't cheat on you, we couldn't help but give him a few pointers." Claire's expression turned serious. "I hope we weren't overstepping."

Maxi shook her head. "No, I think it might help. I feel like we can't go back to the way things were. Something has to change."

"But you are going back." Jane said it as a statement rather than a question.

Maxi paused, her gaze traveling to the bread store. Claire and Rob had a good thing, and Jane and Mike did too. She couldn't imagine starting dating again. She had no desire to do that.

When she'd seen James at the Purple Blueberry, she'd been impressed that he was making an effort. She leaned back in her seat. "Yes, we will get back together, but I want to make it perfectly clear that from now on, I'm going to focus on living my best life. I just hope James can see his way to being a part of it."

CHAPTER TWENTY

ane and Andie stood at the full-length mirror in Jane's room. The inn had been spruced up for the arrival of the wedding guests, but tonight was a night for relaxation and fun before the storm of the guests' arrival.

If only Jane could figure out what to wear.

"What about this one?" Andie pulled a chic black sheath dress out of Jane's closet and held it up to Jane's neck then turned her so she could see it in the mirror.

Jane supposed the dress had potential. It was simple, just the way she liked it, but was it good enough for the opening? What would Mike think of it? Andie, of course, looked like a model in a gray chiffon pantsuit with silvery trim. Her dark hair had been brushed to a silky sheen and flowed down past her shoulders.

"I don't know. It's kind of plain." Jane glanced into

her closet. Maybe she could dress it up with some fancy shoes?

"It suits you. With some simple sparkly earrings and a necklace, it would be stunning," Andie said.

"Maybe." Jane slipped the dress off the hanger and pulled it over her head.

"This reminds me of your freshman prom, when you couldn't decide what to wear." Andie zipped up the back and nodded her approval over Jane's shoulder in the mirror.

Jane smiled at the memory. "You picked out that pretty blue dress, and I got a lot of compliments."

Andie nodded. "I think you look even better now."

Jane turned back to the mirror. She supposed she looked okay. Luckily she had a slim figure, and the dress accentuated that and seemed to make her silvery pixie haircut look modern and chic.

"Those were fun times." Jane turned to Andie. "I miss those times."

"Me too. Simpler times. These last few weeks have been..." Andie's voice drifted off, and she looked away from Jane, out the window toward the ocean. Jane's heart sank. Here it was, the good-bye speech. At least Andie was trying to let her down gently.

Jane picked a pair of diamond stud earrings out of her jewelry box. "It's been great having you here, but I get that you want to go back to work."

Andie turned from the window. "When I first came,

I figured I would bolt after a week like usual. But I wanted to spend more time with Mom, and then there was the garden project, and suddenly this place started to grow on me. And now I've realized that Lobster Bay is where I belong."

Jane turned from the mirror, adjusting the back of the earring. "You mean you're staying?"

Andie's smile widened. "Yep." Then her smile faded. "I hope that's good news."

"Of course it is!" Jane threw her arms around her sister. "We'll fix up your old room and get you some better furniture and—"

"I'm not going to stay at Tides. I don't want to take up a room that could bring income, and besides, I need my own space."

"Oh, of course." Jane felt slightly disappointed, but it made sense. Her sister would want her own place. Maybe she was sick of helping Jane out and would find work elsewhere. The gallery, perhaps?

"Don't worry. I'm still going to help out here with the guests, but there's really not enough for it to be a full-time job."

"Oh. That's great!" Jane said. "What else are you going to do?"

"Well, I've bought an antique store."

"The one downtown that's been closed all this time?" Jane had wondered when someone would buy that.

"Yep. It has an apartment above." Andie told her about meeting Rita and appraising the items for the other women. "So I feel like I can fulfill a need there, and it will be fun. I like helping out here, but I'm chomping at the bit to get back into antiques too."

"Sounds perfect."

The crunch of tires on gravel came through the front-facing window, and they looked outside to see Mike's car pull up.

"Looks like our date is here," Andie said. "You ready?"

Mike was in the foyer. Dressed in a sharp black suit, he looked so handsome it made Jane lose her breath. As they descended the stairs, he looked up. His gaze tracked over Jane, making her feel self-conscious.

"You look amazing."

"Thanks." Andie teased by answering him, though it was clear by the way Mike couldn't take his eyes off Jane that the compliment was meant for her.

"You both do." Mike held out both elbows. "How lucky am I to be able to escort Lobster Bay's most beautiful sisters to the art gallery opening."

Jane took one arm, Andie the other.

"Very," they both said at the same time.

Jane's heart was full. She glanced at Mike from the passenger seat. His smile was relaxed, with none of the stress she thought she'd seen earlier after his mysterious phone call. She truly must have imagined that. She settled back into her seat, happier than she'd been in years. Tonight her best friend was realizing her dream of having an art show, her sister was staying in town, and she was attending the art show on the arm of the most handsome guy in town.

CHAPTER TWENTY-ONE

*J*ames had to admit the Lobster Bay Art Gallery was comparable to any gallery he'd seen in a big city. He knew the opening had happened pretty fast and had expected it to look thrown together, but it didn't. The building was an old mill and had vaulted wooden ceilings and exposed ductwork painted black. The walls had been painted stark white, which highlighted the artwork. The floors were black tile. The front of the building had been reno-vated to have glass windows that rose two stories high.

The space consisted of several large rooms. Dotted around the rooms were four-foot-tall rectangular blocks that held sculptures. The lighting had been aimed precisely to highlight the individual works of art.

It wasn't hard to find Maxi's paintings. In fact, he could tell which ones were hers with a glance. Maybe that was because he knew her so well. He stopped to study his favorite, a sailboat with bright-white sails cutting through the cobalt sea. It was finely detailed and even had little people on board in striped shirts. It was so vivid and realistic he could practically smell the sea air.

"Do you like it?"

Maxi stood beside him, a hopeful, hesitant smile on her lips. She looked radiant in a royal-blue satin dress. Classy plus artsy. He fell in love with her all over again in that moment.

"It's amazing."

A blush crept over her cheeks, making her even more radiant, if that was even possible.

"Thanks." They both looked at the painting, their shoulders touching. "I was out of practice, but I think it came out pretty good."

"Maxi... I'm sorry, I..." James stuttered. All the words he wanted to say got stuck in his throat, and only gibberish came out.

She turned to face him, reached out to touch his arm. "Oh, James, it's not—"

"Maxi!"

Chandler grabbed Maxi's elbow and turned her away from James.

"Excuse me," he said to James then turned back to Maxi. "I have someone you simply must meet."

Maxi shot him an apologetic look as Chandler dragged her away. "Sorry, we can talk later."

James was left staring. What had she been about to say? That it wasn't necessary to apologize because she'd already moved on? His hopes plummeted. She'd rushed off with Chandler and left him there. That said enough, didn't it?

He put his glass of champagne on the next passing tray and left.

❀

Andie wasn't scanning the crowd at the art gallery grand opening for anyone in particular. Certainly not for Shane Flannery. Talking to Jane about high school proms had brought up memories of Shane. She still had vivid memories of how he'd looked the night of their senior prom, still a kid but almost a man. He'd made every-thing magical—an orchid wrist corsage, a limo, dinner at a fancy restaurant then the prom, the beach later.

Oh well, that was all in the past. Andie sighed and sank into the shadows of the ten-foot-tall potted palm in the corner, where she'd retreated to be alone with her thoughts.

As she scanned the crowd, her gaze fell on Jane, Maxi, and Claire. They were clustered around one of Maxi's paintings and looked to be having a great time. Maxi's cheeks were flushed with pride, and Andie felt happy for her. She really was talented, and Andie had heard several of the attendees comment on how vibrant her paintings were. Maxi was going to have a successful career.

Maxi might have been right about Chandler, though. Andie noticed the way Chandler looked at her. Right now he was talking to a group in the corner, but his eyes kept straying to Maxi.

Where was James? Andie had seen him and Maxi talking earlier. It had looked serious, and Andie had hoped they were reconciling. But now she couldn't find him. Hopefully James wouldn't see the way Chandler was eyeing his wife.

The palm tree rustled, and Mike stepped out, his expression registering surprise when he saw Andie.

"Oh, hi. I wasn't expecting anyone to be here." He peered out into the crowd warily as if not wanting to be seen.

"Are you hiding from someone?"

Mike's gaze flicked back to Andie. He sighed. "Sort of. My ex is here, and I think she might not want to be my ex anymore."

"You mean she's still interested in you?" Was that the phone call Jane had been worried about? Protective feelings for her baby sister bubbled up. "Do you return the interest?"

"What? No! That's why I'm hiding back here. She's very... persistent. Practically threw herself at me when she saw me." His gaze went back to the crowd, and his voice softened. "I don't want it to ruin my chances with Jane."

"Which one is she?" Andie knew practically no one there, and she was curious.

Mike pointed his chin toward a blond woman. She looked to be in her thirties, younger than Mike. She was batting her eyelashes up at a tall gentleman. "Looks like she might have found another victim."

Mike let out a breath and leaned against the wall. "Let's hope. I don't know why she's still after me. I broke up with her before I came out here. She usually goes for rich, prominent guys that can help her be seen around town. Not sure what I even saw in her. She's nothing compared to Jane."

Andie turned to study Mike. The guy was clearly distraught. "She usually goes for rich prominent guys?"

"Yeah, she likes the limelight. Sort of a social climber."

"What's her name?"

"Tiffany."

Andie handed Mike her champagne glass. "I think I have an idea that might help you out and also solve another problem at the same time."

The night had been like a dream come true, Maxi

thought, as she stood with Jane and Claire in front of her painting. *Her* painting! Hanging on the wall during an art gallery showing. Just two months ago she would have laughed if anyone told her she'd be standing here now with her two best friends. There was only one other person who she would want at her side.

"Have you guys seen James?" she asked.

"I saw him earlier but not in the last half hour. Did you talk to him?" Jane looked distracted. She was scanning the crowd, probably looking for Mike.

Maxi nodded. "We talked earlier, but Chandler pulled me away to meet one of the art gallery patrons, and I've been looking for him ever since."

"Did you resolve anything?" Claire asked. She was wearing a chic pink tea-length dress that gave her a rosy glow and made her look like she was twenty-five. Or maybe she glowed because she had come on Rob's arm. The two were clearly infatuated. Maxi had watched them as they kept looking through the crowd for each other, Claire's cheeks turning pink every time they locked eyes.

"I think so... not sure. Chandler pulled me away before we had much of a chance to talk. That's why I was looking for him. To finish the conversation."

The dawning realization that James had left dashed Maxi's good mood. If he were here, she would have seen him by now. But why would he come and leave so early? Was it only to tell her what he had started to say? And what, exactly, *had* he been starting to say?

He'd been saying he was sorry. Maxi assumed it was because of the rift between them, though now that she thought about it, James had no reason to be sorry. What if he meant he was sorry that he didn't want to be married anymore? What if her "finding herself" had shown him that he didn't want to be with her? Had she been too selfish and waited too long to make things right, and he wanted out? She wanted her art career, but all of this wasn't worth losing James... What should she do now?

"Who is that woman with Andie?" Claire's question pulled Maxi from her thoughts. Andie was chatting with a pretty blond girl who Maxi hadn't been introduced to. As she watched, Andie flagged down Chandler and introduced the two of them. "I don't know. Maybe one of Andie's antique business acquaintances. That's how she knew Chandler."

"Probably," Jane said. "I forget she has a whole other life and people I don't know in it. Or I guess I should say she *had* a whole other life."

"Had? What do you mean?" Claire asked.

Jane beamed. "Andie's decided to stay in Lobster Bay."

"Oh, that's great!" Maxi was glad. She liked Andie and wanted to get to know her better.

"I think that's a good move. I'm glad for both of

you," Claire said. "Will she be working at Tides? Giving up antiques?"

"Part-time. She's buying the old antique shop on Main Street. The one that's been closed." Jane's eyes narrowed, her gaze directed at the corner of the room. "Is that Mike over by the plant?"

Maxi turned. "Yep. Oh, here he comes. Wonder what he was doing over there?"

Jane shook her head. "Who knows." Jane returned her attention to the group. "Anyway, I'm glad she's staying. Aside from Mom, I don't have any family."

Maxi touched her arm. "I'm happy for you. Andie's great."

"Thanks." Jane smiled as Mike stepped into their circle. "And I'm happy for you. The show is doing really good. Looks like you have a great start to your career."

Maxi glanced at another of her paintings. Five people were grouped around, pointing at it and discussing. That was a good sign. She should just focus on the show and her painting career. But what should she do about James?

James stood at his car, looking at the large windows in the art gallery. Golden light spilled out, and inside he could see shadows of the people mingling. Maxi was one of those people. Was she with that Chandler guy?

They'd been together at the Purple Blueberry, and now he'd dragged her away as if he were a priority. Were they *dating*? The thought made him sick. He couldn't decide what to do. He'd never been a quick thinker. He needed time to mull things over.

Should he go in and tell Maxi how he felt? But he didn't want to make a scene or ruin the show for her, and if she was dating this Chandler guy, then it might not matter how he felt.

"You look glum."

James almost didn't recognize Sally Littlefield without her trademark overalls. Tonight she was wearing a long black skirt and black and tan blouse. She still had the braid, though now it was coiled around the top of her head.

"It's Maxi. I'm not sure she wants me back."

"Really?" Sally tilted her head. "We did a good makeover. Did you go to the Purple Blueberry like we told you to?"

"Yeah, but she was with that gallery owner. Chandler. I didn't stay long."

Sally's eyes narrowed. "Why not? Did she invite you to stay?"

"Yeah... but I felt uncomfortable."

"Uncomfortable? How uncomfortable is it going to feel to *not* be with Maxi at all?"

"Well, when you put it that way..."

"And what about here at the art show?"

"We were talking, and then Chandler came and pulled her away. I didn't know how to take it. Maybe she'd rather be with him."

"I doubt that. He's not her type. You don't have to worry about that. But if you don't do something fast, you might have something to worry about." Sally leaned in close. "You ask me, you're going to have to get out of your comfort zone if you want Maxi back. Now if you'll excuse me, I have some free champagne to drink."

Sally walked off toward the art gallery, and James stood by the car for a few more seconds before getting in and driving away. Get out of his comfort zone? How in the world was he going to do that? He needed time to come up with a plan.

CHAPTER TWENTY-TWO

Why did they all have to check in at once? Jane thought the next morning as she dodged angry aunts and chatty cousins in order to register all the guests who had come for the wedding.

Thankfully she had Andie here to help because Jane doubted she would have been able to referee the argument going on between the bride's feuding great-aunts.

"I will *not* stay on the same floor as her!" Aunt Birdie, a plump woman in her mid-seventies wearing a red polyester pantsuit, crossed her arms over her chest and glared at a shorter woman with a salt-and-pepper bun, who was wearing a pair of navy stretchy pants and a blue flowered shirt.

"Well, I'm certainly not staying on the floor *below* you!" Aunt Gladys huffed.

"Ladies. Would you like some fresh-baked cookies?

We can figure out the room arrangements over here." Andie herded them off to the corner of the foyer where Brenda had set out snacks for the guests' arrival.

"Are they gluten free?" Birdie asked. "I'm allergic to gluten."

Jane turned her attention back to the registrations. The feuding aunts were the least of her worries. She wanted to get the rest of the guests lingering in the foyer checked in before the bride's mother arrived.

The mother, Marilyn, had called earlier to say she'd be checking in around ten thirty and stated in no uncertain terms that she was expecting a full inspection of the premises shortly after she arrived. Judging by her demanding tone, Jane wondered if all the bridezilla's demands had really originated with the mother, as Andie had guessed from talking to them on the phone. Then again, the apple might not fall too far from the tree, and she could be dealing with both a bridezilla and a monster mother of the bride. She just hoped everything they'd done would pass muster.

Brenda came whistling out from the kitchen as Jane finished the last check-in. At least Brenda was enjoying the influx of guests. She'd been happily cooking muffins, breads, and cookies all morning to feed them.

"Well, it's nice to see the inn teeming with guests again," she said as she filled the coffeepot and adjusted the pastries on the tray.

Jane simply smiled at her.

"Boy, that was a challenge getting those two feuding aunts into satisfactory rooms, but I managed to do it. Guess working with difficult antique clients paid off." Andie picked a snickerdoodle off the tray. "It *is* good to see the inn full, though."

Jane wasn't so sure. "Paying guests are always nice."

The crunch of tires on the driveway signaled the arrival of a black sedan. A woman stepped out. She wore a hat with large flowers on it, dark sunglasses, and an expensive Chanel suit.

"Is that the bridezilla?" Brenda whispered.

Jane wiped sweaty palms on her slacks. "No. Worse. It's her mother."

Marilyn Lambert sailed into the foyer, looking over the tops of her sunglasses to appraise the three of them then whipping them off to look around. Her gaze fell on the tray of snacks, and she muttered something that sounded like "pedestrian."

Brenda took in a deep breath. No doubt she was preparing to give Marilyn a piece of her mind, but Andie pushed her back into the kitchen before a fight could break out.

Jane stepped forward and held out her hand. "Welcome to Tides. I'm Jane Miller."

Marilyn gave a limp handshake. "Marilyn Lambert. The place seems... adequate. I'd like a tour of the wedding venue after I check in."

"Of course. Let me get you situated, and then I'll be waiting down here for you." Jane moved behind the desk, dread building in her chest. Pleasing Marilyn Lambert was not going to be easy.

Jane got Marilyn checked into her room and then checked on Cooper, who she'd put in her office in order to keep him from getting underfoot while the guests were arriving.

Andie poked her head in. "Everything going okay?"

"Yes. I'm meeting Marilyn downstairs after she freshens up."

"Need help?"

"Maybe you could help keep Cooper out of sight. It might be best to keep him from running around trying to greet all the guests." Jane would have liked to pawn the job of showing Marilyn around off on Andie, but since she'd been the one to originally book the wedding and talk to Marilyn and Courtney, she felt it was her responsibility.

"Of course." Andie clipped the leash to his collar. "I'll make sure he stays to himself."

Jane got to the foyer at the same time as Marilyn.

"I'd like to see the table-scape, if I may." Marilyn looked at Jane as if she were an indentured servant.

"We have an example out on the back porch." Jane led the way.

"The back porch? I thought there was a tent." Marilyn ran her finger along the surface of a sideboard then inspected it for dust. Jane half expected her to whip out a white glove.

"There will be, but it's being set up tomorrow morning."

Marilyn frowned. "So I can't see the actual setup right now."

"The rental company said that setting it up the morning of the event would be best so that everything is crisp and fresh for the wedding itself. Since it's in the evening, I think that makes sense, don't you?"

"I suppose." Marilyn looked around the room as Jane held the French doors to the back porch open, hoping to distract her with the gorgeous ocean view.

"Luckily it's outside and not in here. So many knickknacks. They collect dust, you know. I hate dust. I like things spic-and-span clean. I don't allow clutter." Marilyn waved toward a sideboard that held Grandma Miller's collection of flow blue plates. "Or pets. Dust and dander are so dirty."

As she swept out onto the back deck, Jane saw Andie disappearing with Cooper on the other side of the inn just in the nick of time.

Thankfully, Marilyn approved of the table setting,

albeit a bit grudgingly. They proceeded to walk across the garden to the bathroom. Jane stopped at the arbor.

"Here's the arbor where the bride and groom will say their vows facing the ocean, and the tent will be directly behind it," Jane said.

Marilyn looked around. "I suppose it's pretty. Those roses are a bit unusual."

"Yes, we worked on the arbor specifically to your daughter's instructions."

"Well, we'll see how she likes it. Now the bathrooms?" Marilyn raised her brows at Jane. "I hope those will be clean and uncluttered, unlike the main house."

Uncluttered? Darn! Jane pictured the starfish and shells she'd placed on the vanities as she led Marilyn toward the building.

❀

Maxi puttered around the cottage, basking in happy memories from the art gallery opening the previous night. Too bad those memories were mixed with worry about James.

She'd been happy with the way her paintings had come out and thrilled at the compliments she'd received, and when she'd seen James, she felt like things were okay between them and all the tension from their misunderstanding had melted away. Then why did he leave?

Rembrandt skittered down the hall, batting a plastic

bottle top in front of him. She knelt and scooped the cat up and held him in her arms like a baby as she talked to him.

"Did I miss the signs with James? I thought he wanted to reconcile, but was he really there to tell me things were over?"

Rembrandt wriggled, and she put him down. He trotted to his food dish.

"And what about that day at the Purple Blueberry?" She got cat food out of the fridge and spooned some into the dish.

James had been seeking her out, she knew. And he'd reached out to Jane and Claire to help him. He'd had a wardrobe makeover, for crying out loud!

No. She was sure he wasn't breaking things off. Something must have made him leave though... Crap! It was because of Chandler, of course. Chandler had dragged her off, and James must have gotten jealous.

She hoped he hadn't gotten the wrong impression, though she was sure that Chandler had been flirty. He'd almost seemed possessive when he'd carted her away.

She'd tried to give off the vibe that she wasn't interested, as Andie had suggested, but her vibe-giving skills were rusty. Though something must have worked, because at the end of the night, he'd been so busy talking to some blonde that he'd hardly even acknowledged Maxi to say good night.

Maxi took out her paints and a fresh canvas.

Painting always helped her think, and she needed to figure out the best way to reconcile with James in a way that would solidify their relationship and not leave a lot of unanswered questions.

❦

"I suppose the building is cute in a commonplace sort of way." Marilyn eyed the bathhouse with a scowl on her face.

Jane bit her lip to remain quiet. Andie and Maxi had put a lot of time into the design, and Jane thought the sailboat shutters and window boxes were quaint. But if Marilyn didn't approve of the outside, she surely wouldn't like the way Jane had set decorative shells and starfish around the inside.

Jane pushed the door open, gesturing for Marilyn to go inside, and closed her eyes, waiting for her words of disapproval.

"Huh, it's very clean. Sparse. I'm surprised, considering how cluttered the house was." Marilyn's praise held a grudging tone.

Huh? Jane opened her eyes and peeked in. Where were the shells that she'd lined up on the vanity? And the dozens of starfish she'd stood upright on the shelves? Had Andie overheard Marilyn taking about dust and clutter and rushed in to remove them?

Marilyn opened each stall door, nodding her approval. Finally she turned to Jane.

"I suppose this will suffice." She glanced out the window. "Courtney should be here soon, and we'll have to show it all to her, but I wanted to have a look at things beforehand so I could try to rectify any shortcomings before she saw them. I don't want my little girl to be disappointed."

"Of course." Jane felt bad for Courtney to have such a meddling mother, though it was nice that Marilyn didn't want her daughter to suffer any disappointment on her big day.

Marilyn led the way outside. She paused at the garden, her gaze resting on the large area to the side where the tent would be set up.

"What about the dance floor?" She narrowed her eyes at Jane as if eager to discover a flaw with the plan.

"That will be set up under the tent. We have a gorgeous wooden floor that will be perfect."

"Oh, well I suppose I can wait to see—"

"Woof!"

Cooper came bounding toward them, his leash trailing from his collar.

Marilyn's eyes widened as the dog brushed past her on his way to Jane's side. He pushed his head under Jane's hand as she grabbed for his leash.

"Is that creature yours?"

"Well, yes... but—"

Andie came around the side of the house, juggling a handful of shells and starfish. That explained where the shells from the bathroom had gone. "Sorry. I had my hands full, and the leash slipped out."

Cooper strained to sniff at Marilyn, and she jumped back. Jane tugged on the leash to rein him in.

"I certainly hope *that's* not going to be here for the wedding!" Marilyn pointed at Cooper.

Apparently Cooper didn't register Marilyn's dislike for him because he wagged his tail and strained to get at her even harder.

"He won't be at the wedding. We'll keep him inside."

"Oh no. This won't do. Not at all. I think—"

"Hey! Mom!"

All three of them swiveled toward the driveway on the other side of the garden, where a young woman waved cheerily. She started toward them, her long honey-blond hair bouncing like in a shampoo commercial as she hurried across the garden. At least she had normal taste in clothes, judging by her plain tan shirt and khaki capris.

Jane's stomach twisted as Courtney hurried toward them. What if their bridezilla hated dogs as much as her mother did?

James woke up determined to get Maxi back. Jane's invitation to the wedding had provided him an opportunity. Sally had said he'd have to get out of his comfort zone, and he knew exactly what to do.

"We'll show her how much we love her, right, Picasso?"

Picasso simply slitted one eye open from his position atop the cashmere sweater vest that James had placed on the bed.

After the hairball incident, James had no desire to wear that sweater again. It didn't go with his new less-fussy look anyway. He'd hand-washed it and then given it to Picasso to lie on. The cat seemed pleased.

James felt nervous about his plan. He'd definitely be out of his comfort zone, but he knew it was something Maxi wanted. And he'd worked hard to gain the new skill that would hopefully prove to her that he had changed and was willing to work toward their relationship. Now if she just didn't show up at the wedding with another date, everything might just work out.

He got his most impressive dress shoes out of the closet and started to polish them. He still had a lot of work to do to perfect his plan and only one day in which to do it.

❧

Jane had expected Courtney to be a sourpuss like her

mother, but she actually seemed rather cheery as she approached the group. On the other hand, she was happy to see her mother, which Jane took as a bad sign because if the two of them were anything alike, she was in for a rough road ahead.

"Great to see you, dear!" Marilyn hugged Courtney and then air-kissed her cheek.

"Hi. I'm Jane. We talked on the phone a few times." Jane stuck out her hand.

"Yes, I remember. Nice to meet you." Courtney's handshake was firm, her smile genuine. Maybe she wasn't so bad after all. "Sorry to be such a stickler on the phone, but Mother wanted everything to be perfect."

Aha! So maybe it was the mother all along.

"Yes, I did. Nothing is too good for my darling daughter." Marilyn sniffed. "But I'm afraid there's a little problem, dear." She nodded toward Cooper.

Courtney's eyes widened, apparently noticing the dog for the first time. "Oh! A dog!"

She crouched down, holding her hand out for Cooper, who was delighted to sniff. Once they were acquainted, Jane eased up on the leash, and Courtney hugged the dog. She looked up at Jane. "Does he live here?"

Jane nodded.

"He's gorgeous. Do you think he could be a ring bearer?"

Stunned, Jane answered, "Sure. He's pretty smart. I'm sure we can train him."

Courtney stood, brushed off her slacks, and hooked her arm through her mother's. "Perfect. Then I guess I'll check in and then take a look at what you have set up for the wedding. The property is lovely, and I'm sure what you have will be just wonderful."

CHAPTER TWENTY-THREE

*J*ane was so busy the rest of the day and into the next that she barely registered the hours ticking by. It turned out that Courtney really wasn't as bad as her mother.

Brenda made a quick ring box and pillow to attach to Cooper's collar, and Courtney helped Andie and Jane train him to walk down the aisle behind her. He learned quickly, but it was one thing to do it with empty chairs and another to do it while the tent was full of guests that could distract him. Jane could only keep her fingers crossed.

The guests all seemed happy, and the couple looked enamored with each other at the small rehearsal dinner held on the back deck of Tides the night before the wedding.

Even the feuding aunts had found common ground.

It turned out they both loved dogs and had tolerated each other's presence, since they both wanted to be near Cooper. Jane had even overheard them reminiscing pleasantly about family dogs they'd had in the past.

When the moment finally came for the wedding, Jane was relieved and somewhat eager to get it over with.

She stood at the back of the tent and watched the couple exchange vows. Cooper stood between them, patiently waiting for the ring exchange.

"See, I knew he'd do a good job." Mike took her hand. "Everything worked out just perfect."

"I guess." Jane watched as the groom kissed the bride, and the crowd erupted in applause. "Now let's hope the reception and dinner goes smoothly."

Several yards away on the beach, the Lobster Bay Clambake Company was tending to the steaming pit they'd dug in the sand and lined with seaweed for the lobsters. Two industrial-sized grills were set up for steak. Waitstaff circled in the tent with trays of hors d'oeuvres as the crowd moved from the seating area to mingle under the tent.

The band had taken their place in the corner and was starting to get set up. Fairy lights twinkled along the edges of the tent. Sheer drapes hung in the corners billowed exotically in the sea breeze. Above the ocean, the first stars were just starting to appear in the cerulean sky.

The guests seemed to be enjoying themselves, and the bride was beaming, which eased some of Jane's nerves. Never having hosted a wedding before, she had no idea if she was doing things right, but so far, so good. Over to the side, she spotted Claire's sand-castle cake. It looked magnificent with its blue sugar-coated icing and really did match the bridesmaid dresses.

"Let's go to the table. I want to tell Claire how much Courtney loved her cake." Jane tugged Mike over to the round table in the back designated for Jane and her friends. Claire and Rob were seated at the table, their heads bent together in private conversation. Maxi sat next to Claire, a champagne flute in her hand as she scanned the crowd.

Andie was standing beside the table talking to the two feuding aunts, who were laughing together about something. Apparently, they'd forgotten about their feud.

Most of the guests were standing in small groups, while a few were seated at the tables. The bride was circulating with the groom in tow. The only person not laughing and talking was Marilyn. She was seated at the head table by herself with a sour look on her face. Jane wasn't surprised about that.

As she approached their table, James came up beside her.

"Wish me luck." He winked at Jane as he went over

to Maxi then took her hand and led her to the dance floor just as the band started to play.

Jane squeezed Mike's hand as she watched the couple. "Ahh, see, you were right. Everything is working out just perfect."

Maxi's heart fluttered as James took her in his arms on the dance floor. James wasn't much of a dancer, but she appreciated the effort.

James looked over at the band and nodded. How odd. Did he know them or...?

They started playing a song she associated with the tango, and James held her hand out in a tango pose. What in the world? James didn't know how to dance the tango.

She played along, shocked when he started to whirl her around in perfect sync with the music.

"When in the world did you learn how to tango?" Maxi had to admit, he was pretty good at it. She'd learned years ago, and her steps were a little rusty, but James was leading beautifully.

James laughed. "You always wanted to take ball-room dancing, and since I'm a klutz, I figured I'd get a head start."

"You took lessons?"

James nodded. Their eyes locked. His were filled

with love and a little uncertainty. She reached up and touched his face. "For me?"

"Anything for you."

"Oh, James, I've been so stupid."

"No, you haven't. You've just been doing what you wanted. All the years you sacrificed to raise the kids, I was too blind to notice that you'd done nothing for yourself. I had my dream career and what I wanted, but you nurtured everyone else at the expense of your own dreams. Now it's your time to do things for *you*." He twirled her away then scooped her back into his arms.

"You mean you don't mind if I paint, or have a cottage studio, or hang out at the Purple Blueberry?"

"Not at all. Well, maybe hanging out at the Purple Blueberry might take some getting used to." He dipped her skillfully. It was impressive how much he'd learned in a short time. How long had he been taking lessons? Surely he wasn't taking them before she left. "I'm hoping I'll be able to join you at all those things."

Maxi's heart expanded. "That would make every-thing just perfect."

He pulled her back in. "Then let's start tomorrow. I have a surprise for you at home."

Maxi raised her brows. "Okay, but first I want to show you my cottage." What would James think of Rembrandt? The old James would have balked at him, but somehow she thought this new James just might be more accepting.

"I can't wait to see it." James pulled her into his arms, and Maxi knew she was exactly where she was meant to be.

⁂

Andie stood on the side of the tent and watched Maxi and James whirl around the dance floor. They looked like newlyweds, and she was happy for them. They were going to be okay.

Her thoughts turned to Jane and Mike. They were seated at the table next to Claire and Rob, the four of them in a lively conversation. At the art gallery opening, Andie had sensed that Tiffany and Chandler had hit it off. Hopefully Tiffany would switch her affections to Chandler and leave Mike alone. Jane was being overly cautious, but Andie knew she and Mike were meant for each other just like Claire and Rob were.

She glanced out at the beach, at Tides, at the bathhouse. They'd pulled the wedding off, and she couldn't be happier. She hadn't thought of her old life in New York once during the past several days. She belonged here. This was her town, and these were her people.

The bride, Courtney, had been ecstatic about what they'd done. Her mother, not so much. But Andie recognized her type, never happy with anything. It was kind of sad in a way, since those types of people always pushed others away. Right now, Marilyn was sitting alone at the head table, stiff backed and pursed lipped, while the rest of the family congregated in groups, talking and laughing.

There was only one creature that didn't seem to be put off by her sour disposition. Cooper. He'd repeatedly tried to make friends, but Marilyn had brushed him off.

She glanced over the crowd again. Most people seemed to be in couples. Even Jane and Claire, who had both been alone for a long time, were in relationships. Maybe everyone had someone out there waiting for them, but was there someone for her? Thoughts of Shane Flannery bubbled up, and she tamped them down quickly. That ship had sailed, and the fact that he hadn't been working at Tides since they'd run into each other there made her wonder if he'd been avoiding her.

"You're looking dreary despite the fact you pulled off this amazing wedding. What's wrong?" Sally wore a gauzy ivory pantsuit, her hair clipped back in a chignon. Andie almost didn't recognize her.

"Oh nothing, just thinking about things." Andie turned her attention to the handywoman. "I didn't know you were coming to the wedding."

"Well, I wasn't invited by the bride or anything. I met Payton over there at the Salty Dog last night, and he invited me." Sally tilted her champagne glass toward a table where a dapper older gentleman in a bow tie sat talking to a younger man. "I never turn down free lobster."

"You look nice." Andie nodded toward Sally's outfit.

"Ayuh. Thanks. I've had enough of this dressing up, though. First the gallery opening then this. I'll be glad to get in my overalls and back to work." Sally appraised Andie. "You look good too. No date?"

Andie sighed. "Nope. Just me."

"Well, at least it looks like things are going to work out for Maxi and James." Sally's gaze followed the dancing couple. "I guess he finally listened to my advice. You know, if people would listen to me more often, they'd be a lot happier."

"I bet they would."

"I have to admit I was a bit worried about that Chandler fellow, though. Seemed like he had a thing for Maxi. But I saw him cozied up down at the Purple Blueberry with a blonde. Not a townie."

"Was she in her late thirties? Shoulder-length hair? Perky?" Andie described Tiffany as best she could.

"Yeah, you know her?"

"Not really. But as long as he's found someone else, that works for everyone."

"Guess so." Sally focused her attention on Andie. "What about you? I hear you're staying in town."

"Yes. This is my home now," Andie said.

"Good. You're the face of Tides now."

"I don't know about that. But this is where my family is, so this is where I'm going to stay." Andie glanced back at the inn. "I'll help with the guests at the inn part-time, and I bought the antique store downtown."

"Good. That's going to work out just perfect for you." Sally scanned the crowd. "And Tides is going to do well. This event is coming off perfectly. I'll bet you get a lot of good reviews. Even that sourpuss Marilyn is softening."

Andie followed Sally's gaze. Marilyn was still seated alone at the head table. Andie watched as she picked a morsel from her plate and leaned down tentatively, clucking to Cooper, who sat at her feet. Cooper's tail wagged furiously, and he put up his paw. Marilyn took the paw as she fed the treat to Cooper, and for the first time since she'd arrived, Andie saw the woman smile.

"Guess dogs bring out the best in everyone." Sally's attention jerked toward the other side of the room. "Payton is motioning me over. Gotta run."

Andie sipped her champagne and watched Sally rejoin her table. She was glad to hear that Chandler and Tiffany had hit it off. It felt good to help people. And now she had a chance to help even more people with their antiques. She couldn't wait to get started.

CHAPTER TWENTY-FOUR

*J*ames approached the front door to Maxi's cottage with a mixture of nerves and anticipation. It was the night after the wedding at Tides, and he and Maxi had picked up where they'd left off. Better than where they'd left off, actually. They were entering a new phase of their relationship. One that he was very much looking forward to.

The cottage was similar to the one he'd looked at with Sandee, and he liked it immediately. He could see Maxi's touches everywhere, from the whimsical wrought iron chair she'd placed out front to the flowers overflowing the window boxes.

Meow!

Picasso voiced his displeasure at being cooped up from inside the cloth cat carrier James held in his right hand. He hadn't told Maxi about the cat and couldn't wait to see the look on her face when he presented Picasso to her.

Palms clammy, he knocked on the door.

The door opened, and there she was. Maxi was wearing a yellow-and-white-checked sundress, and her hair was loose. She looked fantastic.

"Welcome!" She opened the door wider, then her eyes fell to the cat carrier. "What is this?"

James held the carrier out to her. Her smile widened. "Remember when you saw me downtown that day and I tried to avoid you? This is why. It's a present I was getting for you."

Maxi's hand flew to her mouth. "Oh, James, I'm so sorry. I was a fool."

"Never mind that now. It's water under the bridge. We don't need to think about that. Let's focus on the future. Our future."

Maxi smiled, took the carrier inside, and put it on the table.

The inside of the cottage was a little worn, as Maxi had already told him. James liked it anyway, especially since she'd added touches here and there and fixed it up with her usual skill.

Something scampered down the hallway toward him. "You already have a cat?" James sat on the floor and extended his hand to the black kitten, who approached cautiously. "Hey, I think I recognize this little guy. He was at the shelter when I got Picasso."

"Picasso?" Maxi had taken the white kitten out and was cuddling him to her chest.

"I named him after one of your favorite artists. You can change it if you want."

"No, it's perfect." Maxi placed Picasso down next to the other cat and sat on the floor next to James. "This one is named Rembrandt."

Together they watched the two cats circle each other warily. There were a few hisses and a couple of paw swipes, but then they settled in and started playing. Soon they were rolling around in a fluffy flurry of black and white fur.

He stood and brushed a few hairs off his jeans. Oddly, he didn't care as much now about cat hair or appearances. "Looks like they are going to get along fine."

"Almost as if they were meant to be together," Maxi said, her eyes softening as she looked up at him.

"Yes, it is." James took her hand. "Now show me the rest of the cottage and your artwork. I think I'm going to be spending a lot of time here."

❦

Maxi's heart was lighter than it had been in years. But she also felt bad. That day in the street when she'd thought James had avoided her had all been because he was getting her a precious gift.

He should have been mad at her, but here he was, smiling and holding out his hand.

She took it and stood. Keeping her hand firmly in his, she gestured around the cottage. "It's not big, but it works for a nice studio. As you can see, it's not fancy either."

"Who needs something fancy with that view?" James pointed at the beach.

"I know, right?" They had a great view from their house on the cliff, but there was something about being right on the beach and being able to hear the sound of the waves and smell the sea. She pulled him toward the slider and then out onto the patio. "This is my favorite part."

"I can see why." James's gaze drifted from the ocean to the easel setup in the corner. "Is this where you paint?"

Maxi nodded. "I'm going to start a new one tomorrow."

"Excellent. The ones you had at the gallery were amazing. I'm happy for you."

"Really?" Maxi was seeing a new James. He'd always been generous with money and compliments, but he'd never really acknowledged her creative side.

Of course, that might have been because she'd never talked about it. After all, it was she who had abandoned painting, so she couldn't really blame him. She could sense he really was proud and that he wanted her to continue. He wanted to be a part of it. She wondered, though... how far would he go to be a part of her new life?

"I was thinking... maybe later on we could have a drink at the Purple Blueberry," Maxi said shyly.

James's brows rose. "Okay, if that's what you'd like. The place seemed... interesting."

"You don't have to go there if it makes you uncomfortable."

"Uncomfortable? I don't know if I'd say that. It's just not the sort of place I'm used to. But a wise woman told me I have to get out of my comfort zone, so I'd be happy to go."

"A wise woman?"

"Yeah. Sally."

Maxi laughed. "Well, she does like to dole out advice."

"And sometimes it is wise." James pulled her into his arms and kissed her. "She helped me see that I'd become complacent in our relationship. Took you for granted. That's not going to happen anymore."

"Good. Me either."

James looked thoughtful. "You know, getting to know the artsy side of town might not be such a bad idea. Maybe I should institute a lending program for artists down at the bank."

At least James hadn't changed totally. He was still thinking of business, but this time he was mixing it with pleasure. James loved business, and she didn't want him to push that aside for her, but now it seemed like maybe they could both have what they wanted. She could still have James and not lose herself in the process.

❀

One week later...

Andie put the inventory list beside Gloria Farnsworth's silver box on the counter of the antique store. She'd paid nine hundred for the box. That was top dollar, and she'd be lucky to make any profit on it, but the look on Gloria's face when she'd realized the extra money would allow her to purchase horse-riding lessons along with the admission to 4-H camp for her granddaughter was worth it.

The grandfather clock in the corner chimed the hour. Almost time to meet Jane, Claire, and Maxi at Sandcastles for morning coffee. She'd made a dent in the inventory this past week, cataloguing everything in the shop and entering it into her computer. She'd dusted and polished so that everything was in top shape for her opening next week.

The apartment upstairs, on the other hand, still needed work. And furniture. But she could work on all that later. It had been an adjustment moving out of

Tides, but with bookings up, she wanted the room to be empty so they could rent it out.

She grabbed the old skeleton key that locked the front door, stepped outside, then turned and slipped the key into the lock. It was still warm, but the air had that brisk undertone that signaled fall was right around the corner. The leaves were still green, but she pictured how pretty they would be when the tall oaks and maples that lined the street started to turn color.

"Well, hello, stranger." The familiar deep baritone sent her pulse skittering.

Shane Flannery leaned in the doorway of the beauty salon next door. His long legs were crossed, T-shirt stretched across his broad chest.

"Hey, hi," Andie said lamely, trying to act casual. Of all the times she'd looked for him at Tides and when she was running errands around town, he had to come up and surprise her when she was least prepared? She smoothed her hair that she'd shoved into a ponytail atop her head and glanced down at her frayed jeans and dust-covered T-shirt. "Are you doing work in the salon?"

The salon had been busy every time Andie had come to work on her apartment and store. She'd made a mental note to check them out herself. She needed a trim and maybe to cover up some grays. She hadn't noticed any renovations going on, but maybe that was why Shane hadn't been working at Tides.

Shane glanced back into the salon. "No, actually just visiting."

"Oh." Right. His girlfriend probably worked there. Maybe she was the one with the platinum blond bob or the dark curls? Certainly it wasn't the woman with the long gray hair. She looked a good twenty years older than him.

"My aunt, cousin, and niece own it," he said. "Do you remember them?"

Andie's gaze flicked back to the window. She didn't recognize any of them, but it had been decades since she'd met them, and it wasn't like she'd known them well. Just a few meetings at family gatherings. "Oh! Yeah... I mean, I remember them, but didn't realize they owned the shop."

"What are you doing here?" He gestured toward the door.

"I bought the shop and the apartment above."

"Wait. So you're staying in Lobster Bay?"

Did he sound pleased? Andie couldn't tell. Maybe he was just surprised. She couldn't blame him. She'd surprised a lot of people with the decision, including herself and her coworkers at Christies.

"Yep. Gonna help Jane with Tides and run the shop in my spare time."

Shane pushed off the wall, the smile spreading on his face showing off the dimple that always caught Andie's heart. "Well, then, looks like we're going to be seeing a lot of each other. I visit Aunt Mary a couple of times a week."

"Huh, I guess we will, then."

Andie watched him walk to his truck before continuing toward Sandcastles. Yep, it was looking more and more like she'd made the right decision. Despite her feelings of uncertainty at giving up her career and leaving the town she'd called home for most of her adult life, somehow she had a feeling that things were going to turn out just fine for her in Lobster Bay.

****

Find out what happens next in Lobster Bay! Join my newsletter for sneak peeks of my latest books and release day notifications:

https://lobsterbay1.gr8.com

Follow me on Facebook:

https://www.facebook.com/meredithsummers

ALSO BY MEREDITH SUMMERS

Lobster Bay Series:

Saving Sandcastles (Book 1)

Changing Tides (book 2)

Making Waves (Book 3)

ABOUT THE AUTHOR

Meredith Summers writes cozy mysteries as USA Today Bestselling author Leighann Dobbs and crime fiction as L. A. Dobbs.

She spent her childhood summers in Ogunquit Maine and never forgot the soft soothing feeling of the beach. She hopes to share that feeling with you through her books which are all light, feel-good reads.

Join her newsletter for sneak peeks of the latest books and release day notifications:

https://lobsterbay1.gr8.com

❶

This is a work of fiction.

None of it is real. All names, places, and events are products of the author's imagination. Any resemblance to real names, places, or events are purely coincidental, and should not be construed as being real.

MAKING WAVES

❀ Created with Vellum